THE NIGHT WATCHMAN

a bilingual selection of poems

by Yu Kwang-chung

1958-2016

守夜人

中英
對照

余光中 著 · 譯

CONTENTS

目　錄

In Time of Cold War　在冷戰的年代

The White Jade Bitter Gourd 白玉苦瓜

Tug of War with Eternity 與永恆拔河

Dream and Geography　夢與地理

The Pomegranates　安石榴

The Sun Calling His Children　太陽點名

Uncollected Poems　尚未結集

About the Author

Born in Nanking, China in 1928, Yu Kwang-chung is a writer well-known in Taiwan, Hong Kong and mainland China. He has taught English and Chinese literatures at colleges in Taiwan, Hong Kong, and the United States where he was twice Fulbright visiting professor in 1964-66 and 1969-71. He is now professor emeritus at National Sun Yat-sen University in Kaohsiung, Taiwan, where he was dean of college of liberal arts in 1985-91.

A prolific and versatile writer, Yu has published 70 books, of which 18 are in verse and the rest in prose, criticism, and translation. In recent years, 40 books by or on him have been published in mainland China. A dozen or so of his lyrics enjoy popularity as songs, notably "Nostalgia," "Nostalgia in Four Rhymes,"and " Folk Song." Recipient of a dozen major literary awards in Taiwan and China including National Literary Award in Poetry and Wu San-lian Literary Award in Prose, he was conferred honorary fellowship by Hong Kong Translation Society in 1991. He was awarded an honorary doctorate of literature in 2003 by the Chinese University of Hong Kong and the same by Chengchi University and Sun Yat-sen University in 2008.

Critical attention has focused on such verse collections of his as *In Time of Cold War*, *The White Jade Bitter Gourd*, and *The*

Selected Poetry of Yu Kwang-chung. His lyrical essays, ranging in style from the fantastic to the witty, have also won wide acclaim.

The Fire-Fresh Phoenix (1979) and *Five Flying Colors* (1994), edited by Wong Waileung, are selections of critical essays on Yu's poetry and prose. Among Yu's translations are *The Old Man and the Sea*, *Lust for Life*, *Bartleby the Scrivener*, *Anthology of Modern English and American Poetry*, and *Anthology of Modern Turkish Poetry*. His Chinese versions of all of Oscar Wilde's comedies have been successfully staged in Hong Kong and Taiwan. He has also been poet in residence at Peking University and writer in residence at Macao University.

Foreword

Over the past sixty years I have written more than 1,000 poems and translated into Chinese more than 300 foreign poems directly from or indirectly through English. Apart from scattered appearances in anthologies and critical essays, translations of my own poetry have been published only in two books: the German version of Music Percussive by Andreas Donath and the English version of *Acres of Barbed Wire* by myself.

Published both in 1971, the two books are now out of print. However, there has been an increasing need for translations of my poetry on occasions of international exchange. So I rearranged *Acres of Barbed Wire* and enlarged it into the present selection entitled *The Night Watchman*.

This bilingual edition with 68 poems is more substantial than my average collection and amounts to approximately one tenth of my total output in verse. Out of the 68, only 27 are taken from *Acres of Barbed Wire*; the rest are recent translations.

《守夜人》自序

　　寫詩六十多年，成詩一千多首，而翻譯外國的詩，無論是直接譯自英美，或者是間接譯自土耳其，印度、西班牙、匈牙利或南斯拉夫，也有三百多首了。但是自己的詩譯成外文，除了東零西散見於一般詩選和評介之外，成為專書的只有兩本：那便是德國詩人杜納德（Andreas Donath）的德文譯本《敲打樂》（*Music Percussive*），和我自譯的英文譯本《滿田的鐵絲網》（*Acres of Barbed Wire*）。

　　兩書均出版於一九七一年。二十年匆匆過去，Horst Erdmann Verlag所印的德文本，和美亞書版公司所印的英文本，都早已絕版。近年臺灣日趨開放，與國際文壇交流日頻，需要譯本的壓力也顯然日增。我把自己舊譯的《滿田的鐵絲網》加以調整，並大事擴充，成了目前這本中英對照的《守夜人》。

　　這本雙語版的詩集收納了六十八首作品，約占我全部詩作的十分之一，比我一般的詩集份量重些。其中二十七首是沿用《滿田的鐵絲網》的舊譯；至於近二十年來的作品則都是新譯，內有十四首更譯於今年夏天。

A selection of poems in translation is, of course, quite different from ordinary selections of creative writing, where the simple aim is to choose whatever is best and most representative. The former, however, is limited by more complex considerations. Where a poem is unique for its historical background, cultural context or linguistic style, the translator is liable to achieve lamentably less despite painfully greater efforts. Thus I have to excuse myself for having refrained from tackling such demanding yet thankless Muse.

For a poet to translate his own poems, the advantage is, of course, full understanding of the original, there being no risk of misinterpretation. Yet the author, because he knows his own work too well, is often discouraged by the feeling that it is impossible to do full justice to the original in all its subtle nuances so that, as soon as he commits himself to a foreign language, he feels guilty of distortion. To keep my translation from degenerating into prosaic paraphrase, I had sometimes to give verve priority over mere correctness. Since the translator is the author himself, this liberty, I believe, was taken at nobody else's expense.

Yu Kwang-chung
Kaohsiung, Taiwan
Written in August, 1992
Finalized in October, 2016

《守夜人》有異於一般詩選，因為譯詩的選擇有其限制。一般的詩選，包括自選集在內，只要選佳作或代表作就行了，可是譯詩要考慮的條件卻複雜得多。一首詩的妙處如果是在歷史背景、文化環境，或是語言特色，其譯文必然事倍功半。所以這類作品我往往被迫割愛，無法多選，這麼委屈繞道，當然難以求全。也就是說，代表性難以充分。

　　詩人自譯作品，好處是完全了解原文，絕不可能「誤解」。苦處也就在這裏，因為自知最深，換了一種文字，無論如何翻譯，都難以盡達原意，所以每一落筆都成了歪曲。為了不使英譯淪於散文化的說明，顯得累贅拖沓，有時譯者不得不看開一點，遺其面貌，保其精神。好在譯者就是作者，這麼「因文制宜」，總不會有「第三者」來抗議吧？

　　　　　原寫於一九九二年八月，二〇一六年十月修訂於西子灣

Foreword to the Second Edition

Since *The Night Watchman* was published in 1992 I have written more than 300 poems and translated a few of them into English. Seventeen of such translations are now added to the book to bring it up-to-date. With a total of 85 poems now this enlarged edition includes almost one thirteenth of my entire output in verse. I am grateful the Muse in her everlasting youth has not yet forsaken such an old poet as I am.

To remain a poet is to remain young, which gives one the illusion of immortality.

Yu Kwang-chung
Written in July 21, 2004
Finalized in October, 2016

二版自序

　　自從一九九二年《守夜人》出版以來，我又寫了三百多首詩，並英譯了多首。現在將新的英譯加了進去，以展現新的內容。新版一共收詩八十三首，約占我全部詩作的十三分之一弱。感謝永遠年輕的繆思，尚未棄一位老詩人而去。

　　詩興不絕則青春不逝，並使人有不朽的幻覺。

原寫於二〇〇四年七月二十一日，二〇一六年十月（重九）修訂

Foreword to the Third Edition

The Night Watchman was first published in 1992 and then reprinted in 2004. Now another 12 years have passed and this new third edition seems due. Of course this new edition has its changes, with both additions and deletions of about a dozen. The result is still more than 80 poems in this edition, approximately one fourteenth of my total output in verse. Yet there is flexibility in counting the poems, because "Summer Thoughts of a Mountaineer" is a series of 7 poems and "Scenes of Kenting National Park" a series of 11.

Another 12 years will find me a centenarian, but I don't care for being a longevity rarity. So this third edition should remain not only the most recent but also the last edition of *The Night Watchman*.

Yu Kwang-chung
2016

三版自序

　　《守夜人》初版於一九九二年，再版於二〇〇四年，如今又過了十二年；這最新的第三版頗多增刪，增的和刪的各為一打左右。其結果仍是八十多首，約占迄今為止我的總產量十四分之一。不過「首」的認定頗有伸縮，因為這第三版裏收入兩首組詩，例如〈山中暑意七品〉與〈墾丁十一首〉。

　　再過十二年我就一百歲了，但我對做「人瑞」並不熱衷。所以這第三版該是最新的也是最後的《守夜人》了。

二〇一六年

Hsilo Bridge

Loomingly, the soul of steel remains awake.
Serious silence clangs.

Over the Hsilo Plain sea winds wildly shake
This design of strength, this scheme of beauty; they shake
Every nerve of this tower of will,
Howling and yelling desperately.
Still the teeth of nails bite, the claws of iron rails clench
A serious silence.

Then my soul awakes; I know
I shall be different once across
From what on this side I am; I know
The man across can never come back
To the man before the crossing.
Yet Fate from a mysterious center radiates
A thousand arms to greet me; I must cross the bridge.

Facing the corridor to another world,
I tremble a little.
But the raw wind over the Hsilo Plain

西螺大橋

蠢然，鋼的靈魂醒著
嚴肅的靜鏗鏘著

西螺平原的海風猛撼著這座
力的圖案，美的網，猛撼著這座
意志之塔的每一根神經
猛撼著，而且絕望地嘯著
而鐵釘的齒緊緊咬著，鐵臂的手緊緊握著
嚴肅的靜

於是，我的靈魂也醒了，我知道
既渡的我將異於
未渡的我，我知道
彼岸的我不能復原為
此岸的我
但命運自神祕的一點伸過來
一千條歡迎的臂，我必須渡河

面臨通向另一個世界的
走廊，我微微地顫抖
但西螺平原壯闊的風

Blows against me with the tidings
That on the other side is the sea.
I tremble a little, but I
Must cross the bridge.

And tall looms the massive silence,
And awake is the soul of steel.

迎面撲來，告我以海在彼端
我微微地顫抖，但是我
必須渡河

矗立著，龐大的沉默
醒著，鋼的靈魂

Seven Layers Beneath

The wind now ebbs among the pines. The sun sets
West of the Civil War. Only snow garrisons the frontier.
Thin are the bald branches, like starved nerves of the ear.
In the chilled hush the shrubs are listening.

At sunset, the ill-tempered crow in the birch trees
Begins to curse, in dissonant blasphemies,
General Sedgwick with the broken sword.
Startled and strained are the statued ears.

Featured are the rocks; masks hide behind masks.
Soon the cold fog will rise, and under the biotite sky
The dews will nibble the marrow of the guns
In the rusted silence where mildew creeps.

After the war asleep are the stains of blood.
Mute are the bugles, mute the neighing horses that shied.
After the war the vastness of a battlefield
Is listening to a lone, late crow.

七層下

一時松風退濤，落日在內戰以西
殘雪兀自封鎖著邊界
禿柯瘦成聽覺的神經
肅然的寒氣中，灌木叢在傾聽

日落時，壞脾氣的烏鴉
在那邊的樺樹林中咒罵
罵米德將軍斷劍的雕像
百里內，驚動多少耳朵

怪石如顏，鬼面之後有鬼面
不久冷霧泛起，夜空下
露滴侵食鐵砲的骨髓
鏽青了的寂滅中，爬著綠霉

內戰之後，血斑皆酣然
酣然，銅號，酣然，失蹄的嘶馬
內戰之後，一整幅戰場
在靜聽一隻遲歸的鴉

Then Sirius rises from between teeth of battlements.
The weighty sense of Time cumulated falls
On my fatigued collar bone. Also falls
The night, slippery down my icy face.

Softly I tread. Softly, on seven layers of autumn dead,
Seven layers of leaves, crisp and sobbing beneath the shoes,
Till trod and broken lie all the heart-shaped designs,
All the insistences and futilities.

WISDOM SURVIVES PASSION. Ah, exile roaming the
     battlefield,
There is no past for you, no, not a bit.
New Continent is still too new, past there's none for you.
Your past is west of the sunset, west of it.

—Devil's Den, Gettysburg

天狼在雉堞的齒隙升起
累積的時間感，全部的重量
向肩胛骨最痠處壓下
夜色瀉下，沿著誰的冰頰

踏。　踏七層死去的秋
七層枯脆在履底悲泣
踏碎一些心形的圖案
一些多情的執著，一些徒然

太上無情。　古戰場的浪子啊
你沒有什麼往事，沒有一星星
新大陸太新，沒有你的往事
往事在落日以西，唉，以西

　　　　　　　　　　——蓋提斯堡戰場魔鬼穴

27

Smoke Hole Cavern

Pre-historic virgin night devours us,
Such a headless, tailless darkness
Before our life and after our death,
Where, subterranean, blind, cold,
Gargles the trickle of a stream.

We grope upstream along the Lethe
To find the mountain's appendix lead
Nowhere, vaguely aware the sun and moon
Are left revolving somewhere outside.
In whose hand a flashlight

In vain tries to push aside
The impenetrability of it all,
Where a whim-dream has fossilized
Reefs of coral under our feet
And candelabra overhead.

So stalactites fall and stalagmites rise:
So slowly grow Creation's beards.

鐘乳巖

史前的童貞夜嚥下了我們
無首無尾的黑暗
生之前，死之後
冰澗漱著細細的地下水

捫到冥川上游
山的盲腸不通向何方
日月都留在洞外
誰的手中一枝電筒

撥也撥不開的深邃
髮髯凝固的夢境
腳下是珊瑚叢
千盞琳琅是吊燈

石乳下降，石筍上升
盤古的白鬚緩緩地長著

An inch's fall, an inch's rise
While outside, rise and fall the dynasties.
Eternity's where they never meet.

Eternity, eternity! The stalagtites
Whisper to the stalagmites below:
"No hurry for us to grow and meet,
Who knows how many centuries will pass
In this mystery of a sarcophagus?"

A century ago the Confederates,
The guide says, here hid their gold.
And much, much earlier than that,
A feathered and painted Indian chief
Roasted his venison in the cave.

Rocks have their music too, he says
And beats them up and down
And beats them left and right
And upon such a subtle sculpture
Strikes up a pop tune of the Stone Age.

—Smoke Hole Cavern, West Virginia

千載一釐，萬載一分
升降之間虛懸著永恆

永恆，永恆！緩降的石乳
對更緩的石筍耳語：
「何必如此匆匆地相約
我們又何必要終於相遇
在這石槨神祕的世紀？」

百年前，南軍在洞裏藏金
嚮導說，更早更早以前
戴羽繪面的紅酋長
在洞口薰炙鹿肉

岩石也有音樂啊，他說
且揚杖擊石
向玲玲瓏瓏的雕塑敲起
石器時代的流行樂

　　　　　　——西佛吉尼亞·煙洞巖

31

When I Am Dead

When I am dead, lay me down between the Yangtze
And the Yellow River and pillow my head
On China, white hair against black soil,
Most beautiful O most maternal of lands,
And I will sleep my soundest taking
The whole mainland for my cradle, lulled
By the mother-hum that rises on both sides
From the two great rivers, two long, long songs
That on and on flow forever to the East.
This the world's most indulgent roomiest bed
Where, content, a heart pauses to rest
And recalls how, of a Michigan winter night,
A youth from China used to keep
Intense watch towards the East, trying
To pierce his look through darkness for the dawn
Of China. So with hungry eyes he devoured
The map, eyes for seventeen years starved
For a glimpse of home, and like a new weaned child
He drank with one wild gulp rivers and lakes
From the mouth of Yangtze all the way up
To Poyang and Tungt'ing and to Koko Nor.

當我死時

當我死時，葬我，在長江與黃河
之間，枕我的頭顱，白髮蓋著黑土
在中國，最美最母親的國度
我便坦然睡去，睡整張大陸
聽兩側，安魂曲起自長江，黃河
兩管永生的音樂，滔滔，朝東
這是最縱容最寬闊的床
讓一顆心滿足地睡去，滿足地想
從前，一個中國的青年曾經
在冰凍的密西根向西瞭望
想望透黑夜看中國的黎明
用十七年未饜中國的眼睛
饕餮地圖，從西湖到太湖
到多鷓鴣的重慶，代替回鄉

Gray Pigeons

The old guns muse and look afar.
Gray pigeons saunter on the lawn;
An obscure, subdued complaint
Now and then is heard to coo and croon.
On and on through the afternoon
A rosary's told and told and told,
The secret of beads still unknown.
I have a hunch across the sea
There's some one murmuring my name,
Some unseen lips tickling my ear.
Itchy's the ear of afternoon;
The sensitive ear of early dusk
Turns up, with fields full of corn,
And holds a loneliness for miles.
The slow sun does more to chill than cheer,
Dimmed further by pearly clouds.
Under the old guns gray pigeons moan,
A complaint most inarticulate,
Which seems to stammer and hesitate
Off and on through the afternoon.

灰鴿子

廢砲怔怔地望著遠方
灰鴿子在草地上散步
含含糊糊的一種
訴苦，嘀咕嘀咕嘀咕
一整個下午的念珠
數來數去未數清
海的那邊一定
有一個人在念我
有一片脣在惦我
有一張嘴在呵我
呵癢下午的耳朵
下午敏感的耳朵
仰起，在玉蜀黍田裏
盛好幾英里的寂寞
向晚的日色，冰冰
瀰滿珍珠色的雲層
灰鴿子在廢砲下散步
一種含含糊糊的訴苦
含含糊糊在延續

The Single Bed

The moon is a blind man's eye that glowers
At the night through shaggy, unkempt clouds,
Hounded by packs of growling winds.
Look, look up at the firmament
That's freezing into an igloo roof,
Farther than despair, loftier than a dream!
China is more remote than the sun tonight,
When family is remote and friends apart,
And addresses, once so dear, are all forgot.
Loneliness is a single bed
That endlessly extends and extends
Towards the four horizons of the night.
Between the moon and grass I sleep, pillowed
Upon a sorrow undefined, while the wind
Is blowing darkness into a block of ice
And into ashes the passion in my guts,
From which deformed crows, one uglier than the other,
Arise, winging and squawking from my mouth and eyes.

單人床

月是盲人的一隻眼睛
怒瞰著夜，透過蓬鬆的雲
猖猖的風追過去
這黑穹！比絕望更遠，比夢更高
要凍成愛斯基摩的冰屋
中國比太陽更陌生，更陌生，今夜
家人無信，朋友皆遠離
沒有誰記得誰的地址
寂寞是一張單人床
向夜的四垠無限地延伸
我睡在月之下，草之上，枕著空無，枕著
一種渺渺茫茫的悲辛，而風
依然在吹著，吹黑暗成冰
吹胃中的激昂成灰燼，於是
有畸形的鴉，一隻醜於一隻
自我的眼中，口中，幢幢然飛起

The Black Angel

Swift swoops down the Black Angel
From night's innermost navel,
From a sky of setting moon and crows
When wolves are tearing at the crescent
And swarms of rats are nibbling at

The remaining star-crumbs. I am
The Angel of Ill Omen
Who descends at the worst moment
With an obituary telegram
To bang your door and call you up

From amidst your nightmares and sweat.
Among all angels alone I'm black,
An outlaw to every angel white,
And on every black list, long or short,
Most conspicuous you never miss

My name, marked BLACK ANGEL. I am
The black eagle cruising at night:

黑天使

黑天使從夜的臍孔裏
　　飛至，從月落烏啼
　　的天空，當狼群咀嚼
落月，鼠群窸窸窣窣噬盡

滿天的星屑，我就是
　　不祥天使，迅疾
　　撲至，一封死亡電報
猛然捶打你閉門不醒

的惡魘，我就是黑天使
　　白天使中我已被
　　除籍，翻開任何
黑名單，赫然，你不會看不見

我的名字，叫黑天使，我就是
　　夜巡的黑鷹

Through the darkest, the most opaque
Blindness of a moonless, dawnless night
I never discover the best camouflaged

Of evils but will circle over its head
To watch for its last breath of sin
And rush all of a sudden down
Upon its death long overdue,
For I am the Black Angel who never flies

But by himself through lightnings and rain.
To tell the grown-ups fairy tales,
To tell them that God never fails,
The white angels are more than well-paid.
But I am, with a high price on my head,

The Arch-Assassin none can stop
From breaking through the draperies
And rings of guards, from where the night
Is at its most deaf and blind, from outside
The Dark Tower overhanging the Dark Land:

Where the Black Angel strikes, I strike.

最黑最暗的
夜裏，我瞥見最善偽裝的

罪惡，且在他頭頂盤旋
　　等垂斃的前夕
　　作俯衝的一擊
我就是黑天使，我永遠

獨羽逆航，在雨上，電上
　　向成人說童話
　　是白天使們
的職業，我是頭顱懸價

的刺客，來自黑帷以外，來自
　　夜的盲啞的深處
　　來自黲黲的帝國
的墨墨京都，黑天使，我就是

自註：寫成後，才發現這首〈黑天使〉是首尾相銜的聯鎖體，段與
　　　段間不可能讀斷。Emily Dickinson 的 I Like to See It Lap the
　　　Miles 近於此體。

There Was a Dead Bird

When winter solstice's here
And vernal equinox still far,
What dialect is most safe to adopt?
If you're a warbler of a bird,
Beautiful, white all over feathered,
You'll be a taxidermist's delight
To adorn that museum, vivid as if undead.
Under the Latin name will be noted:
A song bird, swift in song and in flight,
Of rare species now, all but extinct.
Or you can sing a timely song
To earn your place in a draped room,
Perched demurely upon a wall,
And pleasing chamber music to make,
Away from the wild woodnote call.
When the clock strikes eleven,
Eleven times, then, must you chime
Under the batons of short hand and long.
Or you will insist on an outdoor song
In the chill-spell of winter when
Sneeze and cough are in tune and safe.

有一隻死鳥

冬至以後，春分以前
哪一種方言最安全？
如果你是一隻鳴禽
美麗，而且有一身白羽
便可以將你剝製成標本
裝飾那家博物館，栩栩如生
拉丁文的學名下，註明
一種鳴禽，能歌，能高翔
罕見的品種，日趨滅亡
或者你可以按時唱歌
堂皇的客廳，棲你在壁上
製造順耳的室內樂，可以亂真
鐘叩七下，你就囀七聲
隨著鐘面的短針，長針
或者你堅持在戶外歌唱
在零下的冬季，當咳嗽
成為流行的語言，而且安全

You insist upon an ear-piercing pitch

Against black blasts of a black night,

No shotgun within range can silence that itch

Not to cough, but to cry in despite

Of the icy blast at your throbbing throat.

No spring is murdered by killing a bird:

A singer dies, yes, but a song never does.

The air never forgets a martyred breath.

Or you can sing on in the teeth of death.

你堅持一種醒耳的高音
向黑色的風和黑色的雲
獵槍的射程內，你拒絕閉口
你不屑咳嗽，當冷飆
當冷飆射進你的熱喉
殺一隻鳴禽，殺不死春天
歌者死後，空中有間歇的迴音
或者你堅持歌唱，面對著死亡

Music Percussive

After the hyacinths and the dandelions,
After the Memorial Day I'm still unhappy,
Unhappy, unhappy, unhappy,
Still carrying on, all by myself,
The unfair argument with existence.
Now I've lost a whole winter
And have lost a whole spring,
Unsure if I won't lose summer after all.

Nettle rash and hay fever,
                              kerchoo!
After the sneeze still unhappy
And unhappy doomed to remain
Unless a miracle comes to pass.
China O China,
When shall we stop our quarrels?

Chianti, and tea bags,
Cold drinks and hot dogs,
Pizzas, raviolis, macaronis, cheese,
Steel the city, cement the road,

敲打樂

風信子和蒲公英
國殤日後仍然不快樂
不快樂，不快樂，不快樂
仍然向生存進行
　　　　　　不公平的辯論
輸掉一個冬季
再輸一個春天
也沒有把握不把夏天也貼掉
蕁麻疹和花粉熱
　　　　　　啊嚏
噴嚏打完後仍然不快樂
而且注定要不快樂下去
除非有一種奇蹟發生
中國啊中國
何時我們才停止爭吵？

奇颺醍，以及紅茶囊
燕麥粥，以及草莓醬
以及三色冰淇淋義大利烙餅
鋼鐵是城水泥是路

After 70-miles-per-hour still unhappy.
After a dinner, unappetizing, cold,
You are an undigested plum,

China O China you are a queue,
Trademark-like trailing behind you.

Always the fancy that afar
There stands a proud tower.
Always the fancy that one at least
Has not yet fallen down to dust,
At least the Five Peaks
Are still supporting the Chinese sky.
Out of a nightmare you yell yourself awake
To find a darker, truer nightmare all around.
Always the fancy
How nice it'd be
On Fifth Avenue to fly a kite,
How nice indeed to have a flute
On top of the Empire State:
On things like that
You muse and meditate.

Always the fancy that come spring you'll take your raincoat off.
Each time you die you shed a skin and more unhappy become.

七十哩高速後仍然不快樂
食罷一客冰涼的西餐
你是一枚不消化的李子
中國中國你是條辮子
商標一樣你吊在背後

總是幻想遠處
有一座驕傲的塔
總是幻想
至少有一座未倒下
至少五嶽還頂住中國的天
夢魘因驚呼而驚醒
四周是一個更大的夢魘
總是幻想
第五街放風箏違不違警
立在帝國大廈頂層
該有一枝簫，一枝簫
諸如此類事情

總幻想春天來後可以卸掉雨衣
每死一次就蛻一層皮結果是更不快樂

After each shave and haircut you look again

Into the mirror at yourself

To see how sorrow again reaps its by-product.

Out of the barber's you come, no happier than when you entered.

China O China you just won't cut or shave away,

You always choke here you're the ulcer that never heals

—The year of Marco Polo Bridge one fancied it's healed.

China O China what a practical joke you've played!

You're a problem, half lost in the cigar smoke of China experts.

They tell me you're raped and overdosed they say you're disgraced,

Deserted, betrayed, insulted, raped again and raped.

China O China you drive me mad.

Washington Monument and Lincoln Memorial

And the Goddess guarding New York rising from the sea.

Thirty six columns raised in the upturned gaze

Raise a self-respect tall and large.

White, pure, hard, every sober block from Colorado,

Not an inch belongs to you, walking down Freedom's steps.

After White House after Manhattan still unhappy,

Still cheerless beyond cure amidst so many cheers.

Dandelions and hyacinths,

Soft is the breeze of May, not for you;

Firm is the marble hall, not for you,

Walking down Freedom's steps.

理一次髮剃一次鬍子就照一次鏡子
看悲哀的副產品又有一次豐收
理髮店出來後仍然不快樂
中國中國你剪不斷也剃不掉
你永遠哽在這裏你是不治的胃病
──盧溝橋那年曾幻想它已痊癒
中國中國你跟我開的玩笑不算小
你是一個問題，懸在中國通的雪茄煙霧裏
他們說你已經喪失貞操服過量的安眠藥說你不名譽
被人遺棄被人出賣侮辱被人強姦輪姦輪姦
中國啊中國你逼我發狂

華盛頓紀念碑，以及林肯紀念堂
以及美麗的女神立在波上在紐約港
三十六柱在仰望中升起
拱舉一種泱泱的自尊
皆白皆純皆堅硬，每一方肅靜的科羅拉多
一吋也不屬於你，步下自由的臺階
白宮之後曼哈頓之後仍然不快樂
不是不肯快樂而是要快樂也快樂不起來
蒲公英和風信子
五月的風不為你溫柔
大理石殿堂不為你堅硬
步下自由的臺階

You're a Jew you're a Gypsy a Gypsy O a Gypsy

Without a ball, you can't tell your fortune at all;

Beyond your sands and your Red Sea there is no God.

Endless go the four lanes, freeways stretch the fifty states.

This is 1966, you're on another mainland.

Three thousand miles dizzy with fast driving from coast to coast,

You take part in the pavement massacre, guilty or innocent,

Stamping over guileful snow and deceiving ice

Headlong into the traps of Easter and the Memorial Day.

The steering wheel is a roulette turning in a wakeful dream towards
    Chicago

Where heaven scrapers press hard upon the angels

And every window opens upon an insurance building or a myth.

The sleek white Dodge,

In the combing wind docile like a snow leopard

That, forward springing, preys fiercely upon the endless scene,

Upon Ohio, Michigan, Indiana, Chicago, Evanston.

This is the far-reaching plain of the Midwest;

Our car wades knee-deep in the green sweetness of the grass

Rippling in the summer breeze and pastoral songs of many
    counties.

In this bread basket are lulled thousands of towns

Slender with chapels, round with water towers, red with farmhouses
    white with pales.

Cattle and sheep are still enjoying grass in Leaves of Grass,

你是猶太你是吉普賽吉普賽啊吉普賽
沒有水晶球也不能自卜命運
沙漠之後紅海之後沒有主宰的神
四巷坦坦，超級國道把五十州攤開
這是一九六六，另一種大陸
三千哩高速的暈眩，從海岸到海岸
參加柏油路的集體屠殺，無辜或有辜
踹踏雪的禁令冰的陰謀
闖復活節闖國殤日布下的羅網
方向盤是一種輪盤，旋轉清醒的夢幻，向芝加哥
看摩天樓叢拔起立體的現代壓迫天使
每一扇窗都開向神話或保險公司
乳白色的道奇
風的梳刷下柔馴如一匹雪豹
飛縱時餵他長長的風景
餵俄亥俄、印第安納餵他艾文斯敦

這是中西部的大草原，草香沒脛
南風漾起萋萋，波及好幾州的牧歌
麵包籃裏午睡成千的小鎮
尖著教堂，圓著水塔，紅著的農莊外白著柵欄
牛羊仍然在草葉集裏享受著草葉

Are chewing clovers and apple blossoms and casual clouds behind
   the barns,
Musing, between dozes, on things guiltless of Vietnam.
They wonder what keeps the bees so busy all through the afternoon.
Hay fever wafts in the air, more popular than the mockingbirds,
When half of America is sneezing in aspirin bottles.
In China (Don't ask me what day this is on the lunar calendar, for
How should I know?) it must be Ch'ing Ming's over and Tuan Wu
   coming,
Ch'ü Yüan's purged, O poor, Left Counsellor!
We have the earliest record of banishing a bard,
(We've had the longest history in the world!)
Earlier than Dante, Hugo, Mayakovsky and many others.
Spacious is the bread basket that feeds most of the States,
Where once troubadoured Whitman, Sandburg and Mark Twain.
Here once I chanted, in my age of anxiety,
On Eliot's dying waste land I once breathed drought. Now the Old
   Possum's dead,
The grass is green again with the green of youth, green from here
   to the Rockies' foot,
And youthful ears inebriate have turned to the West coast,
In the mesmeric rhythm of Bob Dylan have turned to Ginsberg and
   Ferlinghetti.
      From Wichita to Berkeley,
      Down comes T. S. E.,
Up flies Whitman, and Frisco takes all Muses as his brides.
Such kind of weather.

嚼苜蓿花和蘋果落英和玉米倉後偶然的雲
打一回盹想一些和越南無關的瑣事
暗暗納悶，胡蜂們一下午在忙些什麼
花粉熱在空中飄盪，比反舌鳥還要流行
半個美國躲在藥瓶裏打噴嚏
在中國（你問我陰曆是幾號
我怎麼知道？）應該是清明過了在等端午
整肅了屈原，噫，三閭大夫，三閭大夫
我們有流放詩人的最早紀錄
（我們的歷史是世界最悠久的！）
早於雨果早於馬耶可夫斯基及其他
蕩蕩的麵包籃，餵飽大半個美國
這裏行吟過惠特曼，桑德堡，馬克吐溫
行吟過我，在不安的年代
在艾略特垂死的荒原，呼吸著旱災
                          老覷死後
草重新青著青年的青青，從此地青到落磯山下
於是年輕的耳朵酩酊的耳朵都側向西岸
敲打樂巴布・狄倫的旋律中側向金斯堡和費靈格蒂
                從威奇塔到柏克麗
                降下艾略特
升起惠特曼，九繆思，嫁給舊金山！
這樣一種天氣

It's been such kind of weather.

What wind is blowing what flag is up flowing, Weather Bureau?

Shall I put up my flag or everybody's flag?

After all the aspirins

One still coughs and apologetically coughs.

Let's sit with our backs to the wind,

Sneezing each his private sneeze,

Let's talk no more about the weather.

With a zipper let's zip up our souls.

In China this must be the season when breathing is hard

And phosphorous shimmer and shimmer the snail trails.

Around the tombstones what are the mushrooms trying to trace,

 around the tombs

  what are the mushrooms

  trying to trace?

Among the graveyards some beggars are still begging

For leftovers from cold sacrifices.

The thunder may strike the lightning may thrash,

Not a soul will wake and not a single scream

In the month of the yellow plums,

When across the sea I seem to hear

Them cuckoos coo O them cuckoos!

China O China you gi'me the blues.

就是這樣的一種天氣
吹什麼風升什麼樣的旗，氣象臺？
升自己的，還是眾人一樣的旗？
阿司匹靈之後
仍是咳嗽是咳嗽是解嘲的咳嗽
不討論天氣，背風坐著，各打各的噴嚏
用一條拉鍊把靈魂蓋起
在中國，該是呼吸沉重的清明或者不清明
蝸跡燐燐
菌子們圍著石碑要考證些什麼
　　　　　　考證些什麼
　　　　　　考證些什麼
一些齊人在墓間乞食著剩肴
任雷殛任電鞭也鞭不出孤魂的一聲啼喊
在黃梅雨，在黃梅雨的月分
中國中國你令我傷心

Under the clouds freed by Lincoln,
On the grass honored by Whitman,
Sit down before the picnic starts.
China O China you're big in my throat so hard to swallow!
Pessimist of the Orient, I doubt
If still I am young, if young I have ever been.
(To die without ever being young deserves lament.)

After the Memorial Day still unhappy,
Still unhappy quite unhappy never so unhappy.
Chances are no wings whatever will be hatched
If I keep brooding on my grief.
China O China you've hurt me enough.
After the day dark falls the night:
A macabre sense of humor, a grim law.
Strata of overweight sorrow harden into a black mine, jagged,
    packed.
In blind excavation heavily I recline
And erupt myself into a volcanic range.
I am a mainland charged with tension,
Unquenched though Yellow River is drained in quaffs.
I feel my pulse, convinced a heart is not yet dead,
Is still breathing breaths of the thunderstorm;
The Yellow River flows torrential in my veins.
China is me I am China,

在林肯解放了的雲下
惠特曼慶祝過的草上
坐下，面對鮮美的野餐
中國中國你哽在我喉間，難以下嚥
東方式的悲觀
懷疑自己是否年輕是否曾經年輕過
（從未年輕過便死去是可悲的）
國殤日後仍然不快樂
仍然不快樂啊頗不快樂極其不快樂不快樂
這樣鬱鬱地孵下去
大概什麼翅膀也孵不出來
中國中國你令我早衰

白晝之後仍然是黑夜
一種公式，一種猙獰的幽默
層層的憂愁壓積成黑礦，堅而多角
無光的開採中，沉重地睡下
我遂內燃成一條活火山帶
我是神經導電的大陸
飲盡黃河也不能解渴
捫著脈搏，證實有一顆心還沒有死去
還呼吸，還呼吸雷雨的空氣
我的血管是黃河的支流
中國是我我是中國

Her every disgrace leaves a box print on my face I am defaced.

China O China you're a shameful disease that plagues me thirty-
eight years.

Are you my shame or are you my pride, I cannot tell.

I only know you're still a virgin though you've been raped a
thousand times.

China O China you are my qualms!

When O when

Can we ever stop our endless difference

About my cowardliness and your innocence?

每一次國恥留一塊掌印我的顏面無完膚
中國中國你是一場慚愧的病，纏綿三十八年
該為你羞恥？自豪？我不能決定
我知道你仍是處女雖然你已被強姦過千次
中國中國你令我昏迷
　　　　　　　　　　何時
才停止無盡的爭吵，我們
關於我的怯懦，你的貞操？

To the Reader

A thousand stories make one story;
The theme forever same's the theme,
Forever the shame and the glory;
When I say China I only mean
Such as myself and you and him.

致讀者

一千個故事是一個故事
那主題永遠是一個主題
永遠是一個羞恥和榮譽
當我說中國時我只是說
有這麼一個人：像我像他像你

All That Have Wings

China O China what do you want me to say,
A swan without swan-song the songless swan,
An angel without face the defaced angel?
    All are cursed
    That have wings,
Restless and nestless in the wind.
For this is autumn, and all the hearts,
All the maple leaves drift bloody in the wind,
All the asses bray, all the owls hoot.
China O China, even if I want to say anything,
You cannot hear, you will not listen.
For this is winter, and all the hearts,
All the snowflakes drift bloodless in the wind,
All the howling wolves, all the sobbing ghosts.
China O China you cannot hear what I say:
The songless swan unmusical is the swan,
The tearless angel unmoved is the angel.
For out here in the season of the whirlwind
You hear the braying and the hooting and
The frightful laughter and the whining and

凡有翅的

中國啊中國你要我說些什麼？
天鵝無歌無歌的天鵝
天使無顏無顏的天使
旋風旋風在空中兜圈子
　　　凡有翅的
　　　皆被詛咒
在風中漂泊，不能夠休息
況且這是秋天，所有的心
所有的楓葉在風中漂泊
凡驢皆鳴，凡梟皆啼
中國啊中國即使我要說些什麼
你也聽不見你也不願意聽
況且這是冬天，所有的心
所有的雪花在風中漂泊
凡狼皆餓嗥，凡鬼皆哭
中國啊中國你聽不見我說些什麼
天鵝無歌不音樂的天鵝
天使無淚不慈悲的天使
況且在旋風在旋風的季節
況且驢，以及梟，以及其他
以及厲笑的狼以及慘哭的鬼

The Red Guards and the war in Vietnam and
The roll of honor unrolling for miles.
They paste slogans on the face of Li Po.
    The Muses all are butchered
    As sacrifices to the Flag.
China O China what do you want me to say?

以及紅衛兵之外還有越南
以及死亡的名單好幾英里以及其他
以及李白的臉上貼滿標語
殺盡九繆思為了祭旗
中國啊中國你要我說些什麼？

The Double Bed

Let war rage on beyond the double bed
As I lie on the length of your slope
And hear the straying bullets
Like a whistling swarm of glow-worms
Swish by over your head and mine
And through your hair and through my beard.
On all sides let revolutions growl,
Love at least is on our side.
We'll be safe at least before the dawn.
When nothing is there to rely upon,
On your supple warmth I can still depend.
Tonight, let mountains topple and earth quake,
The worst is but a fall down your lowly vale.
Let banners and bugles rise high on the hills,
Six feet of rhythm at least are ours,
Before sunrise at least you still are mine,
Still so sleek, so soft, so fully alive
To kindle a wildness pure and fine.
Let Night and Death on the border of darkness
Launch the thousandth siege of eternity

雙人床

讓戰爭在雙人床外進行
躺在你長長的斜坡上
聽流彈，像一把呼嘯的螢火
在你的，我的頭頂竄過
竄過我的鬍鬚和你的頭髮
讓政變和革命在四周吶喊
至少愛情在我們的一邊
至少破曉前我們很安全
當一切都不再可靠
靠在你彈性的斜坡上
今夜，即使會山崩或地震
最多跌進你低低的盆地
讓旗和銅號在高原上舉起
至少有六尺的韻律是我們
至少日出前你完全是我的
仍滑膩，仍柔軟，仍可以燙熟
一種純粹而精細的瘋狂
讓夜和死亡在黑的邊境
發動永恆第一千次圍城

As we plunge whirling down, Heaven beneath,
Into the maelstrom of your limbs.

惟我們循螺紋急降，天國在下
捲入你四肢美麗的漩渦

The Field Gun

After fifty years in a museum you shall see
This bullying black beast,
Done with curse in his throat, malice in his breast,
And stranded, after the infernal fire and smoke,
The involuntary yelps for help and pain,
Full on history's helpless shore,
A body, unintelligible, of a dinosaur,
Calling more for wonder and pity than for dread.
After fifty years you'll see him in a national park,
A dark massive monster, cleansed of soul's arrogance,
A retired butcher who has long regained
The good humor and unobtrusiveness of old bronze,
Quiet as a monk now in his kindly rustiness.
After fifty years he'll demurely squat
There on the forgetful lawn with the doves,
The unmindful doves cooing in the neighborhood
And festive children astride the barrel imagining
They're riding a giraffe or the steed of a prince.
So young mothers trustingly will lean on him
And prepare their picnics under some olive tree,
Smiling at the camera the unsuspicious smile,

野　砲

五十年後，你將在博物館看見
這尊黑凜凜的巨獸
吐完喉中的敵意，膛中的恨
在火獄和煙網，呼痛和呼救之後
擱淺在歷史無助的岸邊
不可解的一具屍骸，曾是恐龍
幾分可駭，和更多的可笑，可憫
五十年後，你將在國立公園裏看見
這重噸的黑魅，靈魂滌盡驕蠻
一個退休的屠夫，再度恢復
古金屬的好脾氣和純樸
斑斕剝落的慈愛，冷靜如僧
五十年後，他將柔馴地蹲伏
在健忘的草地上，任鴿群
任無知的鴿群在四周沉吟
任孩子們合唱，騎在砲管上，幻想
胯下是長頸鹿，是王子的白馬
任年輕的母親以他為背景
在橄欖樹下準備野餐
而且微笑，向快門與鏡頭

After fifty years, yes, after fifty years,

And never imagine that only fifty years ago

A moment's madness dragged longer than all the centuries,

When with raving monstrosity his lurid arm was raised

In the face of gods and all the tearful angels,

Not an inch to relent or to be dissuaded,

When the savage arm was raised to a blaspheming slant,

Mouth-belching, the curse about to burst.

Your profanity blasted no less loud than truth,

Amidst the smothering smoke spring mud splashed like rain,

Your flashing lectures turned up acres of turf,

Sky stupefied, earth stunned, and faint between your railings came

Coughs of rotten lungs, moans of rotten eyes,

Mothers sobbing, orphans wailing in unisons.

在半世紀，在半世紀之後
而且不了解，在半世紀，在半世紀之前
一分鐘的瘋狂比五十年更長
當暴怒的巨靈啊你的鐵臂舉起
眾神掩面，天使垂淚
也不可勸解，一寸，也不可挽回
鐵臂舉起，成一個褻瀆的斜度
長膛正熱，毒咒在膛中沸滾
你的斥罵宏亮一如真理
濃煙中，春泥飛濺如雨
你大聲呵斥，掀起草皮
天癡，地騃，你大聲喝止
爛肺的嗆咳，爛眼的呻吟
母親低泣，孤兒合唱隊的啼聲

A Cat with Nine Lives

My enemy is not any of the rats, but the whole night,
An attempt to paint everything black
And nibble at the one remaining light.
In the haunted space, listen, twelve strokes
The ancient bronze bell slowly strikes
At the startled heart of midnight, when a sudden blast
With the immensity of a monk's sleeve flaps my face
And down come tinkling the stars, as Death
Puffs out all the birthday-cake candles with one breath.
But Death can't put me out all at once:
My nine lives keep burning nine lamps,
Each casting nine shadows. So I
Am reading a book without an end.
Darkness is an engaging book
I purr alone, from cover to cover.

九命貓

我的敵人是夜，不是任一隻鼠
一種要染黑一切的企圖
企圖噬盡所有的光
被祟的空間，徐徐，十二響
當古銅鐘悚悚敲起
敲響午夜的心臟，忽然有風
寬大的僧袖拂臉過處
星象叮叮噹噹全被掃落，像死亡
一口氣吹熄生日蛋糕的蠟燭
但死亡不能將我全吹熄
九條命，維持九盞燈
一盞燈投九重影，照我
讀一部讀不完的書
黑暗是一部醒目的書
從封面到封底，我獨自讀

Self-Sculpture

How you stand out amidst the whirlwind
And see how madly China whirls around,
Your hair blown where the weather blows
And where the weathercock crows,
With an agonized soberness.
Time is the wind that blows you young
And blows you old and blows off your brows and hair.
How amidst the whirlwind you stand there,
Defiant, a statue of independence,
In a nation that builds no statue for poets:
The pedestal, a massive enough book,
An inspiration that never has shook
Or turned when the whirlwind turned.
How you'd become, in the windy void,
A fixed point because long have you stood.
How, because long have you withstood,
Your garments, one by one, are blown away
And blown everything that adorns,
But that comely gauntliness is yet to come.
How you'd let China, a stone-cutter gone mad,

自　塑

如何你立在旋風的中心
看瘋狂的中國在風中疾轉
鬚髮飛揚，指著氣候的方向
以一種痛楚的冷靜
時間是風，能吹人年輕
能吹人年老，將鬚髮吹掉
如何在旋風的中心，你立著
立成一座獨立的塑像
在不為詩人塑像的國度
像座，是一部堅厚的書
一部分量夠重的靈感
不隨旋風的旋轉而旋轉
如何你在無座標的空間
因立得夠久成一個定點
如何，因為你立得夠久
讓風一件件吹走衣冠
讓風將一切的裝飾吹走
但你仍豐滿，仍不夠瘦
如何讓中國像瘋狂的石匠

Wildly hammer at your agonies,
At all the vanities and cowardliness
Till flake after flake your flesh goes
And through the skeleton your soul glows:
A craggy coral sculptured by the wind.
How China, an aged but ruthless sculptor,
Chops you down into shape.

奮鎚敲鑿你切身的痛楚
敲落虛榮，敲落怯懦
敲落一鱗鱗多餘的肌膚
露出瘦瘦的靈魂和淨骨
被旋風磨成一架珊瑚。　如何
中國將你毀壞，亦將你完成
像一個蒼老，憤怒的石匠

Green Bristlegrass

Who, after all, can argue with the grave

When death is the only permanent address?

When all the condolers have left,

What if the undertaker's back door

Faces the south or the north?

The coach looks always ready for exile,

And none can dissuade it from the trip.

The so-called immortality

May prove nothing but an empty password

For whoever must travel at night,

Even if it works and convinces.

None ends up taller than the bristlegrass

Unless his name soars to the stars

To join Li Po or Rilke

       while the rest

Is left behind beneath the grass.

Keep names to names, dust to dust,

Stars to stars, earthworms to earthworms.

If a voice calls under the night sky,

狗尾草

總之最後誰也辯不過墳墓
死亡，是惟一的永久地址
譬如弔客散後，殯儀館的後門
朝南，又怎樣？
朝北，又怎樣？
那柩車總顯出要遠行的樣子
總之誰也拗不過這樁事情
至於不朽云云
或者僅僅是一種暗語，為了夜行
靈，或者不靈，相信，或者不相信
最後呢誰也不比狗尾草更高
除非名字上昇，向星象去看齊
去參加里爾克或者李白
　　　　　　　　　　　此外
一切都留在草下
名字歸名字，髑髏歸髑髏
星歸星，蚯蚓歸蚯蚓
夜空下，如果有誰呼喚

Who, indeed, is going to answer
Except a glimmer from above
Or a cricket from below?

上面，有一種光
下面，有一隻蟋蟀
隱隱像要回答

If There's a War Raging Afar

If there's a war raging afar, shall I stop my ear

Or shall I sit up and listen in shame?

Shall I stop my nose or breathe and breathe

The smothering smoke of troubled air? Shall I hear

You gasp lust and love or shall I hear the howitzers

Howl their sermons of truth? Mottoes, medals, widows,

Can these glut the greedy palate of Death?

If far away a war is frying a nation,

And fleets of tanks are ploughing plots in spring,

A child is crying at its mother's corpse

Of a dumb and blind and deaf tomorrow;

If a nun is squatting on her fiery bier

With famished flesh singeing a despair

And black limbs ecstatic round Nirvana

As a hopeless gesture of hope. If

We are in bed, and they're in the field

Sowing peace in acres of barbed wire,

Shall I feel guilty or shall I feel glad,

Glad I'm making, not war, but love,

And in my arms writhes your nakedness, not the foe's?

If afar there rages a war, and there we are—

如果遠方有戰爭

如果遠方有戰爭，我應該掩耳
或是該坐起來，慚愧地傾聽？
應該掩鼻，或應該深呼吸
難聞的焦味？　我的耳朵應該
聽你喘息著愛情或是聽榴彈
宣揚真理？　格言，勳章，補給
能不能餵飽無饜的死亡？
如果有戰爭煎一個民族，在遠方
有戰車狠狠地犁過春泥
有嬰孩在號啕，向母親的屍體
號啕一個盲啞的明天
如果有尼姑在火葬自己
寡慾的脂肪炙響絕望
燒曲的四肢抱住涅槃
為了一種無效的手勢。　如果
我們在床上，他們在戰場
在鐵絲網上播種著和平
我應該惶恐，或是該慶幸
慶幸是做愛，不是肉搏
是你的裸體在懷裏，不是敵人
如果遠方有戰爭，而我們在遠方

You a merciful angel, clad all in white
And bent over the bed, with me in bed—
Without hand or foot or eye or without sex
In a field hospital that smells of blood.
If a war O such a war is raging afar,
My love, if right there we are.

你是慈悲的天使，白羽無疵
你俯身在病床，看我在床上
缺手，缺腳，缺眼，缺乏性別
在一所血腥的戰地醫院
如果遠方有戰爭啊這樣的戰爭
情人，如果我們在遠方

The White Curse

How come early snow's already down,

Thin and white above my ears,

And white and thin over the years

When I wore my hair like a proud black crown?

And so the early snow's already here,

So light, though so close to the ear,

That last year, no, even last night, I didn't hear.

No, even this moment I'm not aware

How silently, how beautifully,

How coldly the flakes swirl and swear

Such a pure white curse at my ear,

But invaders are already here and there,

Death's paratroopers borne of the air,

Predicting a storm's about to begin.

And such an early snow, I have heard,

Unlike all other snows in November,

Never, never will melt again,

But will be worse and worse like a growing curse

Until its white malice becomes a blizzard.

And I wonder with such a shudder,

白　災
—— 贈朱西甯

怎麼初雪已然降臨在耳際
薄薄的一層，鋪著殘忍
這樣近，這樣近的冽冽凜凜
怎麼我竟未聽見，雖然雪片啊雪片
這樣向耳邊飄落，飄落白色的咒語
好奇異的侵略，死亡空降的傘兵
預示一場大風雪要開始
而這陣頑固的白雨啊，我知道
將愈下愈大，不可能再融化
最後必然有一座冰峰
標一種海拔的高度，湧起
一種清潔，以零下的肅靜砌成

（僅錄首段）

A lonely victor, how this proud heart of mine,
Will take the dizzy height that's Alpine,
On top of a white whistling crown,
Unable ever to climb home and down.

Sense of Security

The land is old and sprawling, yet the climate
Is still wayward and wild.
From the typhoon that turns and turns
And with it five thousand years
Of nightmares and fitful naps
No single corner is secure
Save in the center of the threat
—The typhoon's eye, blue and fair,
Lashed on all sides by the storm.
In our time every mind
Is an exception of its kind.
Let whoever tries to rise
Above the lightning and the thunder
Reach himself far and out
Into the commotion of the skies
Where only the elements rule.
In our time every pen
That stays straight is a special pen.
Every lightning rod is sure
None dies of war who goes to war.

安全感

土地蒼老，氣候猶多變而年輕
直徑五千年的大颱風
沒有一個角落是安全
除了危險的中心
—— 那颱風眼，金髮，藍瞳
一千層威脅繞，繞它在中間
在我們這時代
每個人都是例外
誰要超越電殛和雷懲
讓他伸出自己
向黑猙猙的風雨
最可怖的禁區
在我們這時代
每一枝筆是一個例外
每一枝避雷針都相信
敢於應戰的，不死於戰爭

Often I Find

Often I find my youngest daughter sitting out on the veranda
And gazing, in enchantment, at the garden in early spring,
Now lisping something quite meaningless to herself,
Now smiling guilelessly at some nameless thing.
From where I watch her I can hardly see
What exactly it is she's looking at,
But from the reflection in her eyes I'm sure
The world she envisions is fairer than the world I see.
Once, like this child, I also had
A childhood, overshadowed by the Red Sun Flag,
A childhood dark with endless roads, hulky trucks and boats,
With dogs barking and nights when lights were out
And eternity dripping indifference by itself
Deep in the slimy air-raid shelter where fitfully we slept.
Light there was in the eyes of a child of war,
But what's reflected was fire, not the sun. O how I hope
The girl's memory will prove more beautiful than mine,
And the world she takes from her father as a gift
Will look more like a toy than my father's gift.

時常，我發現

時常，我發現最小的女兒，在陽臺上
向早春的花園怔怔出神，時而
無意識地喃喃自語，時而
向一些不知名的什麼傻笑
從我坐的角度我看不清楚
她眼中所見的究竟是什麼
但從她眼中的反光，可以確定
她所見的世界比我的要美麗
曾經，像這個女孩，我也有過
太陽旗遮暗的，一段童年
記憶裏有許多路，許多車，許多船
許多狗叫，許多停電的夜晚
和陰濕的防空洞深處
地下水一滴滴如斷續的永恆
抗戰的孩子，眼中，也曾有反光
但反映的不是陽光，是火光，我希望
這女孩的回憶比我的要美麗
希望她父親送給她的這世界
比我父親送給我的更像玩具

Chimney Smoke

—on seeing a dance with
zither accompaniment

"Evening must be tired," says the zither. "It is yawning.
Evening is stretching in purple drowsiness.
The woodcutter must come home now, home from the mist;
So must the fisherman, home from the stream.
    On earth supper's ready says the breeze,
    In heaven the gods sniff and sneeze.
Chimney smoke is an ethereal cry;
Some one's waving evening good-bye;
Chimney smoke is chimney's song
    The kitchen god sings in his niche
    And patron gnome in his notch,
Till stars peep and peer in rivers and lakes,
And Lord of the Clouds says in his clouds:
'It's late now, time for you all to go to bed!'
So chimney curls, or straight or slant,
All chimney curls are called upstairs,
Are called upstairs, are called upstairs."

炊　煙

　　── 劉鳳學舞，張萬明箏

「想黃昏是倦了，」那古箏說
「黃昏在呵欠
黃昏在遠方伸淡漠的嬾腰
想此刻正歸來樵夫，歸自雲霧
也應有漁父歸來，歸自波濤
　　　人間飯香
　　　天上仙饌
炊煙是一聲空渺的呼喊
炊煙是誰在向黃昏揮手
炊煙是煙囱吟一首小令
　　　土地公哼一哼
　　　灶神吟一吟
吟到滿地江湖，滿天是星斗
雲中君是雲中的仙人，說
時間不早了呢，該上來睡覺了呢
說著，就把所有的炊煙都召上樓
都召上樓，都召上樓去了」

Thirteen twanging strings, none takes flight.
Silent the zither, the candle, the girl in white.

十三根弦，一根也不曾飛去
箏留下，燭留下，白衣的少女

　　本詩發表在《中國時報》〈人間〉副刊時曾有下列一段附言：
　　右詩一章，余光中先生所寫。他把這首詩抄寄給我，並附短
柬，文曰：

　　　　昨夕與內人同賞劉女士製舞發表會，歡喜讚歎，目為之
　　明，神為之爽，附上小品一首，請轉呈劉張二女士，以表敬
　　意。

　　光中對藝術製作向不作輕許，他的批評，可稱「月旦」。杜
工部詠公孫大娘劍器舞，運用最精美的文字，傳達舞蹈的形式和
內容，成為千古絕唱。光中又一遭顯示文字功能，而且顯示了語
體的傳達功能。
　　「黃昏在遠方伸淡漠的嬾腰」，是劉鳳學的舞蹈語言，張萬
明的指頭私語，余光中的生花妙筆，羽化了「曖曖遠行人，依依
墟里煙」。

　　　　　　　　　　　　　　　　　　俞大綱附識　　五月十一日

A Coin

Once I tightly held a coin in my hand,
Which an old baker gave me as change,
An old coin with an image worn flat and dim.
Faintly, it seemed to smell of something foul,
Half of well-thumbed copper, half of sweat,
Made all the worse by a film of grease.
For a moment I could hardly decide
If such a filthy trifle I should take,
But the old man had raised his greasy hand,
A trusting smile rippling over his trenched face,
And in spite of myself I opened my hand,
And, plop, the coin was already in my palm.
O it was so assuring to the touch,
And up through my palm a warm stream swelled
Flooding into my heart, I did not know
If with it a schoolboy had just paid his bus,
A girl had flipped for her first date, a worker
With smeared fingers a fried roll had bought.
I only knew the coin would be mine awhile
And soon with a stranger would be gone.
I held it tight, sweat, grease, everything,

一枚銅幣

我曾經緊緊握一枚銅幣，在掌心
那是一家燒餅店的老頭子找給我的
一枚舊銅幣，側像的浮雕已經模糊
依稀，我嗅到有一股臭氣
一半是汗臭，一半，是所謂銅臭
上面還漾著一層惱人的油膩
一瞬間我曾經猶豫，不知道
這樣髒的東西要不要接受
但是那賣油條的老人已經舉起了手
無猜忌的微笑蕩開皺紋如波紋
而我，也不自覺地攤開了掌心
一轉眼，銅幣已落在我掌上
沒料到，它竟會那樣子燙手
透過手掌，有一股熱流
沸沸然湧進了我的心臟。　不知道
剛才，是哪個小學生用它買車票
哪個情人用它來卜卦，哪個工人
用汗黑的手指捏它換油條
只知道那銅幣此刻是我的
下一刻，將跟隨一個陌生人離去
我緊緊地握住它，汗，油，和一切

And seemed to shake hands with all mankind.
I had thought all values were mine to judge:
Hundred dollars worth a hundred, a coin, a coin,
Had seemed a ready and obvious truth
Until that cold morning I stood in the street,
Lost, with a coin burning in my hand.

像正在和全世界全人類握手
一直以為自己懂一切的價值
百元鈔值百元，一枚銅幣值一枚銅幣
這似乎是顯然又顯然的真理
但那個寒冷的早晨，我立在街心
恍然，握一枚燙手的銅幣，在掌心

The Death of a Swordsman

They planted chrysanthemums on his tomb.
Each October, in the slow, soft sweetness,
Came the black-veiled man to the tomb,
Kindled incense, knelt, and let tears gush,
Speechless, from fast closed eyes,
Hot tears that scorched the chrysanthemums.
The husky figure left alone, but
Would come again next year when autumn came.
At last fell an autumn without the man,
And nothing remained except stars of vivid yellow
Like nobody's soul left naked by itself.

                    Says the old monk,
The swordsman was murdered, not defeated:
Some say poisoned, some, circulation-stopped;
And so he fell, eyes open, hacked to death.
Since then his sword's been mysteriously lost
—His sword, never unsheathed unless for justice,
But once bare, an ugly life must cease to be,
The icy steel must flash in a bloody spree;

一 武士之死

他們在他的墓上種了些菊花
每到十月，遲緩的清芬中
就出現那蒙面人在墓前
上香，下跪，讓淚水從閉住的眼中
流下，灼熱的淚水燙痛菊花
然後飄飄離去，然後
第二年和秋天一同來上墳
終於有一個秋天不見那蒙面人
數叢鮮黃留下，像誰的
魂魄，淒涼給自己看。　那老僧說
武士是害死的，非戰死的
有人說是點穴，有人說用砒霜
眼睜睜被亂刀剁死，後來
他的劍就神祕地失蹤
—— 他的劍，從不為不義出鞘
出鞘，必斷卻一醜陋的生命
冰冷的鋼必有次痛飲

Sore was he who fell, grave he who stood,
Thrilled the crowd, awed and hushed, that stood around.
—His sword, says the monk, has disappeared
Since his death. For the sword was the man,
And the man, the sword, neither could live alone.
Death is a ritual to unsheathe the soul:
When it's done, only the rusty sheath remains.

              And now in mid-air
An overshadowing giant sword seems to hang,
Its blue blade glaring, haunting all them cowards,
Along whose chilled necks night after night
Cold sweat drips through dream after bad dream.

仆者痛，立者肅其容，觀者大快
—— 他的劍，那武士死後
就神祕地失蹤，那劍是那人
那人是那劍，人死，劍亡
死，是靈魂出鞘的一種典禮
禮成，只留下生鏽的劍鞘
而一柄無形的巨劍似懸在半空
青鋒眈眈，崇著一切奸徒
夜夜冷汗，滴，沿一個冰頸的惡夢

The Death of an Old Poet

What is life except a flag out there on the very front:
With wind on one side, and rain on the other,
Flapping up into a desperate song
The inarticulation of the weather?
If on this side sets the moon,
Wouldn't on that side croak the crows?
Whatever ventures into the void
Is never scared of nothingness.

    It's been always like this:
If on this side is celebration
On that then must be preparation
For dirges and a funeral.

    In the end always the conclusion:
A place is unsafe if unthreatened by war,
And every standing point is
A stopping and a starting point,
Where some boot-prints end, others begin.
And the flag, that rose with the bugle,
That rose with the outbursts of the bugle,

老詩人之死

所謂生存不過是最前線的一面旗
正面是風反面是雨
招招展展拍響拍不響的天氣
這邊月落那邊就烏啼
敢探向虛空的就不怕空虛
　　　總是這樣
這邊要慶祝那邊就準備舉哀
　　　總是這樣的結論
最安全的地帶是戰爭的地帶
任何一個立足點
是終點，也是起點
有的靴印只到此，有的，從此地開始
旗啊，在號聲中升起
在急驟的號聲中升起的

Will slowly fall, down along the golden call
Amongst hushed salutations of all upturned eyes.
And so will slowly fall
A battered flag to be his pall,
A brocaded honor, an emblazoned going home.

將緩緩下降，隨金黃的號聲
下降，最高的注目禮紛紛，下降
一面破旗，蓋在他身上
一件錦衣，一種赫赫的榮歸

I Dreamed of a King

—on a painting by Wang Lan

I dreamed of a king, a blue-eyed king,

Tall and gaunt, with hair so black and long

Over the shoulders hanging.

From spring O from cool, cool spring

Came he, from misty, misty spring and dim.

From amidst the ancient mist of spring sadly came he,

Sadly came he, the blue-eyed King.

—They took him down from the cross;

Then the withered frame itself turned into spring,

The loveliest O of all the season the loveliest olive tree.

And there in the ancient spring mist dreamed I

Of a colored and unearthly light

That turned from years of war to years of peace,

From hate to love. With hair so black and long

Over his shoulders hanging, I dreamed of a king,

Tall and gaunt, a King of Heaven,

Who roamed on earth O on earth roamed he.

我夢見一個王
── 題王藍同名水彩畫

我夢見一個王，藍眼睛的王
高高瘦瘦，那樣黑那樣長的頭髮
垂在肩上。　自春天青青的春天
他走下來，自迷迷啊濛濛的春天
古春天的霧裏，憂鬱地走下來他
走下來，那藍眼睛的王啊
── 人群將他抱下，從十字之上，
後來，那枯木架子也變成春天
最可愛，春天最可愛的一樹橄欖
古春天的霧裏，夢著，我夢著
五彩而奇怪的一種光輝
在旋轉，戰爭的年代向和平
恨向愛。　那樣黑那樣長的頭髮
垂在肩上，我夢見，高高瘦瘦
一個王，天上的王，在地上流浪，在地上

Alone On the Road

Your pair of shoes, how many streats can they kick?
Your feet, how many pairs of shoes can they wear?
Your breath, how many towns can it swallow?
Your life, how many red lights can it run?
    The answer, O the answer
    Is blowin' in the wind.

Your eyes, how long can they burn?
Your mouth, how many cups can it kiss?
Your hair, how many combs can it survive?
Your heart, how ever youthful can it be?
    The anser, O the answer
    Is blowin' in the wind.

Why always, the letter flies over the clouds?
Why always, the ticket remains in your hand?
Why always, nightmare haunts your pillow?
Why always, you're hugged by a coat?
    The answer, O the answer
    Is blowin' in the wind.

江湖上

一雙鞋，能踢幾條街？
一雙腳，能換幾次鞋？
一口氣，嚥得下幾座城？
一輩子，闖幾次紅燈？
　　答案啊答案
　　在茫茫的風裏

一雙眼，能燃燒到幾歲？
一張嘴，吻多少次酒杯？
一頭髮，能抵抗幾把梳子？
一顆心，能年輕幾回？
　　答案啊答案
　　在茫茫的風裏

為什麼，信總在雲上飛？
為什麼，車票在手裏？
為什麼，惡夢在枕頭下？
為什麼，抱你的是大衣？
　　答案啊答案
　　在茫茫的風裏

A stretch of mainland, can you call it your country?
A lonesome isle, can you call it your home?
A fleeting wink, can you call it your youth?
A fleeting life, can you call it forever?
     The answer, O the answer
     Is blowin' in the wind.

一片大陸，算不算你的國？
一個島，算不算你的家？
一眨眼，算不算少年？
一輩子，算不算永遠？
　　答案啊答案
　　在茫茫的風裏

自註：本詩的疊句出於美國年輕一代最有才的詩人與民歌手巴
　　　布・狄倫的一首歌〈Blowin' in the Wind〉。原句是The
　　　answer, my friend, is blowin' in the wind / The answer is
　　　blowin' in the wind.「一片大陸」可指新大陸，也可指舊大
　　　陸：新大陸不可久留，舊大陸久不能歸。

A Folk Song

By legend a song was sung in the north
By the Yellow River, with her mighty lungs.
From Blue Sea to Yellow Sea,
    It's heard in the wind,
    And heard in the sand.

If the Yellow River froze into icy river,
There's the Long River's most motherly hum.
From the plateau to the plain,
    It's heard by the dragons,
    And heard by the fish.

If the Long River froze into icy river,
There's myself, my Red Sea howling in me.
From high tide to low tide,
    It's heard full awake,
    And heard full asleep.

If one day my blood, too, shall freeze hard,
There's the choir of your blood and his blood.

民　歌

傳說北方有一首民歌
只有黃河的肺活量能歌唱
從青海到黃海
　　風　也聽見
　　沙　也聽見

如果黃河凍成了冰河
還有長江最最母性的鼻音
從高原到平原
　　魚　也聽見
　　龍　也聽見

如果長江凍成了冰河
還有我，還有我的紅海在呼嘯
從早潮到晚潮
　　醒　也聽見
　　夢　也聽見

有一天我的血也結冰
還有你的血他的血在合唱

From type A to type O,
　　It's heard while crying
　　And heard while laughing.

從A型到O型
　哭　也聽見
　笑　也聽見

The Begonia Tattoo

Long have I forgot why a little scar
Marred my left chest, had forgot
When it took its place there:
  Was it made by a sword
  Or a dagger,
  Or some one's soft lips
  That bit a kiss into a curse?
Until one day, well past my youth,
The day when my heart began to ache,
When in my mirrored nakedness I found
That scar, no longer a little scar,
But the vivid print of a vicious palm,
A bloody crab, a brand of begonia tattoo.
Stupefaction! Look at the ugly distortion
And tell me if
The bleeding image of a wound
Is hacked from without
Or burnt from within.

海棠紋身

一向忘了左胸口有一小塊傷痕
為什麼會在那裏，是刀
挑的，還是劍
削的，還是誰溫柔的唇
不溫柔的詛咒所吻？
直到晚年
心臟發痛的那天
從鏡中的裸身他發現
那塊疤，那塊疤已長大
誰當胸一掌的手印
一隻血蟹，一張海棠紋身
那扭曲變貌的圖形他驚視
那海棠
究竟是外傷
還是內傷
再也分不清

Passing Fangliao

Listen, listen to the rain
Falling flush on Pingtung's plain,
On Pingtung's fields of sugar cane.
The sugary rain on the sugary plain,
How the sugar canes suck
The juicy rain in the juicy fields.
The rain falls flush in Pingtung's fields.
From here to the distant hills
How the fertile plain lulls
The canes, the sweet hope of the canes.
My bus whizzes across the green,
Greeted by the green guards of Pan,
While I wonder what cane he dozes under,
The shaggy and bearded god.

Listen, listen to the rain
Falling flush on Pingtung's plain,
On Pingtung's fields of watermelon.

車過枋寮

雨落在屏東的甘蔗田裏
甜甜的甘蔗甜甜的雨
肥肥的甘蔗肥肥的田
雨落在屏東肥肥的田裏
從此地到山麓
一大幅平原舉起
多少甘蔗，多少甘美的希冀
長途車駛過青青的平原
檢閱牧神青青的儀隊
想牧神，多毛又多鬚
在哪一株甘蔗下午睡

雨落在屏東的西瓜田裏

The sugary rain on the sugary plain,

How the watermelons suck

The juicy rain in the juicy fields.

The rain falls flush in Pingtung's fields.

From here to the distant shore

How the cradle sands rear

The melons, the swelling hopes of the melons.

My bus whizzes across the sands

In view of the fecund hoard of Pan,

While I wonder what melon he sits on,

The sanguine and seedy god.

Listen, listen to the rain

Falling flush on Pingtung's plain,

On Pingtung's fields of banana.

The sugary rain on the sugary plain,

How the banana trees suck

The juicy rain in the juicy fields.

The rain falls flush in Pingtung's fields.

甜甜的西瓜甜甜的雨
肥肥的西瓜肥肥的田
雨落在屏東肥肥的田裏
從此地到海岸
一大張河床孵出
多少西瓜，多少圓渾的希望
長途車駛過纍纍的河床
檢閱牧神纍纍的寶庫
想牧神，多血又多子
究竟坐在哪一只瓜上

雨落在屏東的香蕉田裏
甜甜的香蕉甜甜的雨
肥肥的香蕉肥肥的田
雨落在屏東肥肥的田裏

The rain is a swishing shepherd's song,
The road is a slender shepherd's flute
Fluting miles of paddy paths.
The rain falls flush in banana fields,
Plump the bananas plump the rain.
My bus never outruns the openness of Pan.
The road is an endless shepherd's flute.

We're saying Pingtung's the sweetest of counties
And the town must be built with sugar cubes when,
A sharp right turn, the saltiest,
A shock slap on the face, look,
The sea!

雨是一首濕濕的牧歌
路是一把瘦瘦的牧笛
吹十里五里的阡阡陌陌
雨落在屏東的香蕉田裏
胖胖的香蕉肥肥的雨
長途車駛不出牧神的轄區
路是一把長長的牧笛

正說屏東是最甜的縣
屏東是方糖砌成的城
忽然一個右轉，最鹹最鹹
劈面撲過來
那海！

Building Blocks

How amazing to find, now the poem's written,

The rain has stopped all of a sudden!

They must all be asleep, the world below.

I'm all alone up in the tower,

Lofty solitude is ultimate.

The passage of twenty years

Finds me still playing poetry,

A game of building blocks with words.

But such a game is too sad,

Played only by oneself,

When childhood playmates have grown mature

And would no longer share

A game that never grows old.

Ultimate loneliness is all my own

And twenty years find me still in the game,

Still convinced such blocks,

If built solid enough and tall,

Would one day so steadfast stand

No child's play could ever upset:

Nothing is so fast

As towering solitude.

積　木

詩成，才驚覺雨已經停了
全睡著了吧下面那世界
連雨聲也不再陪我
就這樣一個人守在塔上
最後的孤獨是高高的孤獨
── 二十年後，依然在寫詩
搭來搭去，依然是方塊的積木
只是這遊戲
一個人玩未免太淒然
從前的遊伴已經都長大
這老不成熟的遊戲啊
不再玩，不再陪我玩
最後的寂寞注定是我的
二十年後，依然在玩詩
依然相信，這種積木
只要搭得堅實而高，有一天
任何兒戲都不能推倒
一座孤獨
有那樣頑固

Nostalgia

When I was young,
Nostalgia was a tiny, tiny stamp,
Me on this side,
Mother on the other side.

When I grew up,
Nostalgia was a narrow boat ticket,
Me on this side,
Bride on the other side.

But later on,
Nostalgia was a lowly grave,
Me on the outside,
Mother on the inside.

And at present,
Nostalgia becomes a shallow strait,
Me on this side,
Mainland on the other side.

鄉　愁

小時候
鄉愁是一枚小小的郵票
我在這頭
母親在那頭

長大後
鄉愁是一張窄窄的船票
我在這頭
新娘在那頭

後來啊
鄉愁是一方矮矮的墳墓
我在外頭
母親在裏頭

而現在
鄉愁是一灣淺淺的海峽
我在這頭
大陸在那頭

The Telephone Booth

A glass cell that cuts more than it connects,
That often jails me in
And tortures my nerves numb
With a shrill, impersonal monotone,
While desperately to the receiver I hold on
As to a severed umbilical cord.
What number, after all, can I dial?
And who do I want to answer my call?

I've only wanted to dial me out,
Out of this box they call a booth,
Out of this booth they call a town,
Out of these drawers, these apartments, out!
And dial in sounds of wind,
And sounds of water,
And sounds of birds,
And the twilight green hush of the woods.

電話亭

不古典也不田園的一間小亭子
時常，關我在那裏面
一陣淒厲的高音
電子琴那樣蹂躪那樣蹂躪我神經
茫然握著聽筒，斷了
一截斷了的臍帶握著
要撥哪個號碼呢？
撥通了又該找誰？

不過想把自己撥出去
撥出這匣子這電話亭
撥出這匣子這城市
撥出這些抽屜這些公寓撥出去
撥通風的聲音
撥通水的聲音
撥通鳥的聲音
和整座原始林均勻的鼾息

The Call

Just as, in my childhood,
Across that field of flowering rapes
Behind the old house,
I trotted on and on till dark,
When sun was set and cold was sweat,
And seemed to hear from afar
Mother's voice calling me
To come home for supper,

Imagine how in my age,
When sun is set and cold is sweat,
There from the house of 5000 years
A lamp by the window is lit
And a voice is heard,
Even more soothing and moving
Than in my childhood,
Calling me to come home.

呼　喚

就像小的時候
在屋後那一片菜花田裏
一直玩到天黑
太陽下山，汗已吹冷
總似乎聽見，遠遠
母親喊我
吃晚飯的聲音

可以想見晚年
太陽下山，汗已吹冷
五千年深的古屋裏
就亮起一盞燈
就傳來一聲呼叫
比小時更安慰，動人
遠遠，喊我回家去

The Night Watchman

This side of the five thousand years a lamp still burns,
After forty a pen is still erect.
Of all weapons this is the last.
Even if surrounded three times
At the center of blind darkness,
This I will never surrender.
In the forsaken cemetery of Time
Not a stone door ever answers my pounding,
But, hollow with horror, the haunting echoes
Down Time's hallway peal from end to end.
How much chaos will give way to a single lamp?
Does my pen at middle age suggest
A daring sword or a pitying crutch?
Am I the driver of the pen or the driven?
Am I the giver of the blood or the given?
Not a question can I answer. I only know
Icy is the air on the hair of my nape.
The last watchman by the last lamp
To prop a giant shadow awry,
Too preoccupied to dream
Or a sound sleep to claim.

守夜人

五千年的這一頭還亮著一盞燈
四十歲後還挺著一枝筆
已經，這是最後的武器
即使圍我三重
困我在墨黑無光的核心
繳械，那絕不可能
歷史冷落的公墓裏
任一座石門都捶不答應
空得恫人，空空，恫恫，的回聲
從這一頭到時間的那一頭
一盞燈，推得開幾呎的渾沌？
壯年以後，揮筆的姿態
是拔劍的勇士或是拄杖的傷兵？
是我扶它走或是它扶我前進？
我輸它血或是它輸我血輪？
都不能回答，只知道
寒氣凜凜在吹我頸毛
最後的守夜人守最後一盞燈
只為撐一幢傾斜的巨影
作夢，我沒有空
更沒有酣睡的權利

Beethoven

—ever since eighteen hundred and two
he's turned a deaf ear to the world's din.

The soul of commanding wrath never dies,
For some of the living do not let him.
Some ghost-scared people do not believe
The giant spirit would lie back in the grave
Or the children's ears could hold out against
The whirling echoes after his death.
How often at night do frightened fists
Pound the door?   Can the ghost-scared chant
A little red book into a curse
From the first to the fifth nightly watch,
Shouting every oath to dispel their fear,
All sorcerers hurling their dark spells
To drown out the master's magnificent voice?
Hoofs, shells, trumpets of Napoleon's host,
Can these, raging a hundredfold, repel
The shock of a death-mask, of glaring eyes,
Of irrepressible locks in wilful flight?
And the will, the undaunted will belongs

貝多芬

──一八零二年以後
他便無聞於噪音

憤怒的幽靈從來不死去
有一些生者不讓他死
有一些怕鬼的人不相信
魁梧的魂魄肯伏在墓裏
不相信孩子們的耳朵能抗拒
身後，他漩渦不斷的回聲
驚拳搗門，一夜是幾遍？
怕鬼的人從三更到五更
把一本紅皮小冊子念成符咒
叫吼所有的咒語來壯膽
所有的巫師齊誦經文
能不能淹沒宏大的樂音？
拿破崙的蹄聲，號聲，砲聲
千倍萬倍的鼓譟能不能嚇退
赫然一張死面，目光厲閃如電
虬指的亂髮矯矯飛旋
那意志，亢昂不屈那意志

Not to the German but to all the free

Who walk freely at night, unscared of ghosts,

Of Confucius, of Franz and Amadeus.

The fearless fear no haloed heads.

Let the haunted dig out all the graves

And whip back from the living to the dead.

But never will die the tameless soul,

For whoever holds the whip won't let him die.

Trembling you are, you whipping hand;

The shade is not in the grave but in your mind.

Wet and cold sweats the insomnia fiend

Whose heart is a mad drum, listen, who's at the door?

Fate's first phrase thundering four lightning claps,

Who, after twenty-five years, who's at the door?

不屬德意志，屬自由的人
不怕鬼的人，坦坦夜行的人
不怕仲尼，不怕法朗慈和亞馬狄斯
所有戴光冕的人都不怕
讓怕鬼的人翻開所有的墳墓
一鞭從今人打到古人
驍悍的幽靈從來不死去
揮鞭的人不讓他死
揮鞭的手，你顫抖，揮鞭的手
鬼不在墓裏，在你心裏
冷汗濕，失眠症的患者
鼓聲是心悸，聽，誰在擂門？
命運第一句，霹靂四個重音
二十五年的緊閉後，誰，在捶門？

The White Jade Bitter Gourd

—seen at the Palace Museum, Taipei

Seeming awake yet asleep, in a light slow and soft,
Seeming, idly, to wake up from an endless slumber,
A gourd is ripening in leisureliness,
A bitter gourd, no longer raw and bitter
But time-refined till its inner purity shows.
Entwined with bearded vines, embowered with leaves,
When was the harvest that seems to have sucked,
In one gulp, all that old China had to suckle?
Fulfilled to a rounded consummation,
Palpably, it keeps swelling all about,
Pressing on every grape-bulge of creamy white
Up to the tip, tilting as if fresh from the stem.

Vast were the Nine Regions, now shrunk to a chart,
Which I cared not to enfold when young,
But let stretch and spread in their infinities
Huge as the memory of a mother's breast.
And you, sprawling to that prolific earth,
Sucked the grace of her sap through root and stem
Till the fond-hearted mercy fondly reared,

白玉苦瓜

—— 故宮博物院所見

似醒似睡，緩緩的柔光裏
似悠悠醒自千年的大寐
一隻苦瓜從從容容在成熟
一隻苦瓜，不再是澀苦
日磨月磋琢出深孕的清瑩
看莖鬚繚繞，葉掌撫抱
哪一年的豐收像一口要吸盡
古中國餵了又餵的乳漿
完美的圓膩啊酣然而飽
那觸覺，不斷向外膨脹
充實每一粒酪白的葡萄
直到瓜尖，仍翹著當日的新鮮

茫茫九州只縮成一張輿圖
小時候不知道將它疊起
一任攤開那無窮無盡
碩大似記憶母親，她的胸脯
你便向那片肥沃匍匐
用蒂用根索她的恩液
苦心的悲慈苦苦哺出

147

For curse or for bliss, the baby bitter gourd
On whom the mainland lavished all her love.
Trampled by boots, hard trod by horses' hoofs,
By the rumbling tracks of heavy tanks,
There it lies, not a trace of scar remains.

Incredible, the wonder behind the glass,
Still under the spell of blessing earth,
Maturing in the quaint light all untouched
By time, a universe ever self-contained,
A mellowness beyond corruption, a fairy fruit
From no fairy mountain, but from our earth.
Long decayed your former self, O long decayed
The hand that renewed your life, the magic wrist
That with shuttling glances led you across, the smile
When the soul turned around through the white jade
A song singing of life, once a gourd and bitter,
Now eternity's own, a fruit and sweet.

不幸呢還是大幸這嬰孩
鍾整個大陸的愛在一隻苦瓜
皮靴踩過，馬蹄踩過
重噸戰車的履帶踩過
一絲傷痕也不曾留下

只留下隔玻璃這奇蹟難信
猶帶著后土依依的祝福
在時光以外奇異的光中
熟著，一個自足的宇宙
飽滿而不虞腐爛，一隻仙果
不產在仙山，產在人間
久朽了，你的前身，唉，久朽
為你換胎的那手，那巧腕
千眄萬睞巧將你引渡
笑對靈魂在白玉裏流轉
一首歌，詠生命曾經是瓜而苦
被永恆引渡，成果而甘

The Kite

—for Fang-ming across the Pacific

Eager for the exotic, an aspiring kite,
Its light tail flapping and trailing,
By a west wind is blown up the sky,
Up the sky, wind-wafted far and high.
Slim and thin, does the single thread trace
All through the elemental space?
Fierce the wind and foul the weather,
Threatening to snap altogether,
Does the fading thread still hold?

The speck of a kite, free among the clouds,
Should not forget to come back home:
Winging with the cloud-clan is not for life.
Viewed from below, it also seems to ride supreme,
Its flowing sleeves almost a cloud,
Yet, on closer look in the void of the sky,
A cloud is a cloud, and a kite a kite;
A mock bird, remember, is no real cloud,
While in the wide coldness of space

放風箏
—— 隔水寄芳明

好高鶩遠，躍躍有一隻鳶
輕飄飄的尾巴曳著
一陣西風，便吹上了天
吹上了天，愈吹愈渺遠
一條線，嫋嫋細細可牽著？
穿進濛鴻，可依然貫著？
那樣悍的風那樣的氣象
似斷似不斷
一絲悠悠可依然挽著？

那鳶影，逍遙之遊在雲間
該不忘回家來
雲族霞裔該長非伴侶
從下面望上去，也乘風高舉
翩翩仙袂儼然一片雲
而茫茫的天上，近看
霞是霞，孤鳶是孤鳶
該不忘自己是假鳥，不是真雲
而那樣闊冷冷的空虛

The thread of hope that sent it up,

No, the single thread of chance to grasp

Is tied, not to the clouds, but to the earth.

送它上去的一線希望
不，唯一可握的那一線生機
繫於地上，不繫於雲間

The Pole-Vaulter

The pole-vaulter all resilient is a superman.
Of three things he must be sure:
When does the pole touch the ground?
When does he take off in flight?
And when does he let it go,
The pole that sends him to the top?

Quick and powerful, the pole
Shoots him up in air
Where he kicks himself,
Feet first, into an arc and,
    Twisting his waist,
    Turning his torso,
    And releasing the pole
At the zenith of his success,
    Tipsy yet alert,
Comes lightly back to earth.

撐竿跳選手

那富於彈力的選手他是位超人
有三點他必須看準：
何時長竿刺地？
何時奮身一縱起？
送他上去那長竿，何時該拋棄？

敏感而強勁，顫顫那長竿似弓
將他激射向半空
他將自己倒蹴
精巧地蹴成一道弧
──而旋腰，迴身，推竿
凌空一霎間，在勝利的頂點
他半醒半醺飄飄然降回地面

The Power Failure

Suddenly, in silence comes the monster
And, with one lick of its black tongue
Snatches the heart of civilized West.
So gone is the sick heart of America:
Hushed and dead lie all the engines;
Paralyzed, the elevators and the subway;
Blinded, all the traffic and neon lights.
Where on earth are you, New York?
The stunned angels cry amid the stars.

For twenty-five hours raves the Dark Age.
Plunder, you Vandals and Goths!
All dark alleys lead to Rome.
Plunder! Not for hunger but for gain,
Not black and white TV but color TV.
And all amid the doomsday din,
Who are passing candles in the square
—clear dots of light,
So kind yet so frail like some lost rite?

大停電

那怪獸，它來時迅快而無聲
　黑舌一舔
就噬去西方文明的心臟
美利堅多病的心臟它噬去
所有的機器都停下，死去
癱瘓了地下鐵痲痺了電梯
盲掉，所有的交通燈，霓虹燈，廣告
紐約你怎麼不見了
驚起星際的天使，都哭道

廿五小時，降下新黑暗時代
搶吧，汪達爾人哥德人
每條暗巷都通向羅馬
搶，不為麵包，為機器
黑白電視機換彩色電視機
末日的囂嚷中
是誰在廣場上分贈蠟燭
　點點清光
溫柔而微弱如失傳的古禮？

When Night Falls

Once I looked through the harbor's costliest shops
Just for a graceful desk lamp
With a firm stand, a slim upright post,
And a classical shade trimmed with lace,
Like a parasol soft with yellow halo
To offer me such gallant shelter
Against the night, the dark downpour
Of the night. Just for a cozy lamp
To share night after windy night
All in the privacy of fellowship.
For when night falls, the lamp stands on my side
And history is out there on the night's side,
While in between the endless whirlwind blows.
Is night, then, for the bed or the lamp?
Is it with the asleep or with the awake?
In the end will always come a time
In utter silence and solitude to face
Whispering ghosts up on the walls, to face oneself
And shoulder all the dark weight of night.
The asleep are launched on a thousand pillows
To be ferried to a thousand dreams.

蒼茫來時

曾經，走遍這海港最華貴的街道
只為找一盞靈秀的檯燈
燈臺要穩，燈柱要細而修挺
燈罩要繡典雅的花邊
華蓋如傘，一圈溫柔的黃暈
那樣殷勤地遮護著我
不許夜色，哎，黑漓漓的夜色
將我淋濕。　一盞脈脈的檯燈
多少風夜要共我分擔
依依相守最親密的陪伴
蒼茫來時，燈總在我的一邊
歷史，在暮色的一邊
無窮的迴風，吹，在中間，而夜
是屬於床呢還是屬於燈？
是屬於夢著的還是醒著的人？
天邊地廓總有個時辰
靜了萬籟要單獨面對
四壁的鬼神啾啾，要面對自己
要獨當夜深全部的壓力
睡者頭枕一千隻方枕
千枕渡千般不同的世界

The awake keep watch over the same night
That closes in on us, and in ceaseless silence
It seems we've been sleepless thousands of years.
And the lamp by the elbow, candle's child
And torch's remote heir, seems to have shone
Through the long night that spans the centuries.
Yet, however deep the night and sound the snore,
A few lamps will always shine and drill
Holes through darkness in echo to the stars
Before the birth of patriarch torch.

醒者守的是同一個夜
從四壁壓來，永寂裏
髮髯幾千年都未曾睡過
而肘邊這盞燈，燭光的孩子
火把的遠裔，髮髯幾千年的長夜
也未曾熄過，而無論多夜深
四面鼾息多酣多低沉
總有幾盞燈醒著燦然
把邃黑扎幾個洞，應著
火把誕生前荒老的星穹

Listening to a Bottle

Always had I imagined that all bottles

Were empty and mindless

Until one day I leaned to a bottle's mouth,

Suprised to hear the whole world

Whirling and whirling inside

Into a rounded perfect song,

Just as the clear serenity

That settles to the bottom of my mind

Was but the world's turbulent din

That fell whirling and dashing

Shrill against my victim ear.

聽瓶記

一直以為全世界所有的瓶
都是空的，無所用心
直到有一天俯向瓶口
驚聞全世界所有的聲音
都在瓶底迴盪又迴盪
聽不厭，隱隱渾圓的妙響
亦如我心底澄澈的寧靜
原是舉世滔滔
逆耳旋來的千般噪音

Tug of War with Eternity

Surely I am doomed to lose,

Tripped across the line, man and rope:

So the game ends

— One more round of unfair contest.

But the powerful foot on the other side

Occasionally just may slip

And over the line just may step

To print the miracle

Of just one, even half a footprint.

Yet in the dark no one knows

What's at the other end of the rope

That pulls taut and tough as night goes on

Until one's dragged tottering across.

So under the wind-bestirred stars

Against eternity I hold my ground

All by myself through the night.

與永恆拔河

輸是最後總歸要輸的
連人帶繩都跌過界去
於是遊戲終止
── 又一場不公平的競爭
但對岸的力量一分神
也會失手，會踏過界來
一隻半隻留下
腳印的奇蹟，愕然天機
唯暗裏，繩索的另一頭
緊而不斷，久而愈強
究竟，是怎樣一個對手
跟蹌過界之前
誰也未見過
只風吹星光顫
不休剩我
與永恆拔河

The Crystal Prison

—on watch

Uncountable unless under a magnifying glass,
Such dutiful and skillful little slaves,
Carried with care by tiny nippers only:
By what mischievous spirits, from where,
And with what tricks, were you kidnapped
To this curious device of a crystal prison?
Shut behind the round steel gate, waterproof,
Day and night, to a pressing beat push
Around the center of quietude,
Push all the golden wheels of a mill
That grinds the heartless flow of centuries
Into years and months, days and hours,
And hours into fine flour of minutes,
Of minutes and moments and seconds.
So out drips it all, by stealth, through the gate
Called "waterproof." This is the tiniest
Of plants, that, tick-tock-tick, knows no rest.
If you doubt it, gently press your ear
Down to your wrist and listen intent
To the slaves' songs in the crystal prison,

水晶牢

——詠表

放大鏡下彷彿才數得清的一群
要用細鉗子鉗來鉗去的
最殷勤最敏捷的小奴隸
是哪個惡作劇的壞精靈
從什麼地方拐來的，用什麼詭計
拐到這玲瓏的水晶牢裏？
鋼圓門依迴紋一旋上，滴水不透
日夜不休，按一個緊密的節奏
推吧，繞一個靜寂的中心
推動所有的金磨子成一座磨坊
流過世紀磨成了歲月
流過歲月磨成了時辰
流過時辰磨成了分秒
涓涓滴滴，從號稱不透水的閘門
偷偷地漏去。　這是世界上
最乖小的工廠，滴滴復答答
永不歇工，你不相信嗎？
貼你的耳朵吧，悄悄，在腕上
聽水晶牢裏眾奴在歌唱

Time's ever chewing, gnawing monotone
When wheels meet wheels, teeth fitting zigzag teeth.
Are the prison songs, you ask, happy or sad?
Happiness or sadness is all yours to feel.
The turning wheels, listen, are neither sad
Nor happy, even though rivers flow
From your wrist. Gently put your ear down
To the two pulses racing day and night,
Warm blood racing against cold steel,
Blood running faster, seventy to sixty.
At first the young blood led at hundred and forty,
The care-free rabbit leaping far ahead,
But the steely steps are closing in.
Lay your ear to your wrist and, listening, tell
Which pulse is the beat of your life.

應著齒輪和齒輪對齒
切切嚼時間單調的機聲
眾奴的合唱，你問，是歡喜或悲哀？
歡喜或悲哀是你的，你自己去咀嚼
悲哀的慢板和歡喜的快調
犀利的金磨子，你聽，無所謂悲哀
不悲哀，縱整條河流就這麼流去
從你的腕上。　輕輕，貼你的耳朵
聽兩種律動日夜在賽跑
熱血的脈搏對冷鋼的脈搏
熱血更快些，七十步對六十
最初是新血的一百四領先
童真的兔子遙遙在前面
但鋼的節奏愈追愈接近
貼你的耳朵在腕上，細心地聽
哪一種脈搏在敲奏你生命？

A Tale on the Hill

Sunset says, behind the dark writhing pines,
That ebb tide of a burning cloud
Is the signature he left
Changing from fiery red to ashy purple,
Valid for the evening only.
Some homeward birds
Flying over for a closer look
Are soon lost in the twilight, no, the dark
With not a bird coming back:
This tale is most prevalent
In autumn among the hills.

山中傳奇

落日說黑蟠蟠的松樹林背後
那一截斷霞是他的簽名
從焰紅到爐紫
有效期間是黃昏
幾隻歸鳥
追過去探個究竟
卻陷在暮色，不，夜色裏
一隻，也不見回來
── 這故事
山中的秋日最流行

Teasing Li Po

You were once the Yellow River pouring from heaven,
    That shook the Ying Mountains
    And flung open the Dragon Gate,
But now Yellow River comes flooding from your lines,
    Surging and foaming in laughter
    All the way into the sea.
Is the cataract that rocks Mount K'uang,
    Falling out of nowhere,
    Pouring down from midair,
    Your little wine pot tilting?
The Yellow River comes from the west,
The Yangtze goes on to the east,
Or else the five thousand years
Would be all a reign of silence.
The Yellow River is pomp enough for you,
Leave the Yangtze to youngster Su.
    Let all the waves be divided
    Equal between the bards of Shu:
    You on top of Dragon Gate,
    He in command of Red Cliff.

戲李白

你曾是黃河之水天上來
　　陰山動
　　龍門開
而今黃河反從你的句中來
　　驚濤與豪笑
　　萬里滔滔入海
那轟動匡廬的大瀑布
　　無中生有
　　不止不休
可是你傾側的小酒壺？
黃河西來，大江東去
此外五千年都已沉寂
有一條黃河，你已夠熱鬧的了
大江，就讓給蘇家那鄉弟吧
　　天下二分
　　都歸了蜀人
　　你踞龍門
　　他領赤壁

Mosquito Net

On midsummer night in my boyhood,
Childish dreams were made all in milk-white gauze.
The mosquito net hung lightly sloping down,
Nebular with fine little holes in tapestry,
Already mesmeric to the sleeper below.
The dream-catching net was all too thick
To admit a bloodthirsty assassin in flight,
The black-clad, bedaggered night traveler
Who kept complaining and whining outside,
Yet thin enough to let moonlight in
And tree shadows. And so in the timidity
Of piping insects a curl of mosquito incense
Lured me into a meandering dream...until

Blinking, I woke up
In a bed half fiery red with sun beam.

紗　帳

小時候的仲夏夜啊
稚氣的夢全用白紗來裁縫
圓頂的羅帳輕輕地斜下來
星雲鬘鬘的纖洞細孔
仰望著已經有點催眠
而捕夢之網總是密得
飛不進一隻嗜血的刺客
── 黑衫短劍的夜行者
只好在外面嚶嚶地怨吟
卻疏得放進月光和樹影
幾聲怯怯的蟲鳴裏
一縷禪味的蚊香
招人入夢，向幻境蜿蜒──

一睜眼
赤紅的火霞已半床

Autumn Equinox

In September, when eagles are sharp-eyed
And frost and dew are all vigilant,
How sunshine, never rusty since its birth,
Flashes golden like a magic sword
That early above the east horizon
Is unsheathed all across the sky
And raised so upright and so high,
Yet higher and higher to the zenith of Fall,
While below, all clock-towers keep raising their arms
Until they point to the very apex.
Then all the ritual bells start ringing,
And in a golden flash comes down the sword
When, precise as a geometer, God
Severs autumn with one slash,
Equally, into day and night.

秋　分

鷹隼眼明霜露警醒的九月
出爐後從不生鏽的陽光
像一把神刀抖擻著金芒
絕早便在東方的地平線
光動長空地赫赫然出鞘
愈舉愈高，愈高愈正
再高上去，高上去，到秋的頂點
地上，所有的鐘樓都高舉雙手
到不能再崇高的方位
萬鐘齊鳴的典禮
金芒一動，刀光霍霍落處
精確似幾何學家的神
把晝夜就這麼斷然平分
——了秋色

The Umbrellas

What a darkening squadron of baleful bats,
Blind, with baffled squeaks!
You black-cloaked clan
Hanging upside down,
Unable to lift yourselves, even in flight,
With all your ribbed wings, thinly drawn.
Like so many spirits surprised by spring,
In a thunderstorm you flutter about,
In twos and threes,
From behind every door in every shadowed house.

雨　傘

黑湫湫的一大群蝙蝠
喑啞又盲目
展盡你骨稜稜的翅膀
也只能貼地飛的
倒掛的烏衣幫啊
像眾魂驚醒於清明
一陣大雷雨
便從家家戶戶的門背後
三三兩兩
迎面撲來

To Painter Shiy De Jinn

They told me that when summer came
You would go on a long, long trip
To see van Gogh or Hsü Pei-hung,
With your easel and graying hair
And your laughing Szechwan accent.

You would leave Taipei empty, my friend,
Never a backward glance down the lanes.
Another rainy season has set in,
Black with umbrellas, yellow with mud:
Why can't you wait until mid-autumn?

Only the fields in the South will stay,
Those crumbling temples, those buffaloes.
When summer evening falls, my friend,
There always will be egrets, two or three,
That, recalling something, hover up

As if from your vivid ink-painting.

寄給畫家

他們告訴我，今年夏天
你或有遠遊的計畫
去看梵谷或者徐悲鴻
帶著畫架和一頭灰髮
和豪笑的四川官話

你一走臺北就空了，吾友
長街短巷不見你回頭
又是行不得也的雨季
黑傘滿天，黃泥滿地
怎麼你不能等到中秋？

只有南部的水田你帶不走
那些土廟，那些水牛
而一到夏天的黃昏
總有三三兩兩的白鷺
彷彿從你的水墨畫圖

記起了什麼似地，飛起
　　　　　—— May 28, 1981, 廈門街的雨巷

Evening

If evening is a lonely fort,
The west gate open to sunset glow,
Why are all the travelers,
Who hurry on horseback,
Allowed only a passage out
And never an admission in?
And, once out, they're all ambushed,
When sunset clouds switch to black flags
And the west gate shuts behind.
Often I turned to ask the garrison,
But was answered only by bats
Flitting up and down an empty fort.

黃　昏

倘若黃昏是一道寂寞的戍關
西門開向晚霞的豔麗
匆匆的鞍上客啊，為何
不見進關來，只見出關去？
而一出關去就中了埋伏
晚霞一翻全變了黑旗
再回頭，西門已扃閉
──幾度想問問堞後的邊卒
只見蝙蝠在上下撲打著
噢，一座空城

Summer Thoughts of a Mountaineer

I. A Pine Cone Falls

A pine cone comes stealing down
With no notice at all.
Who is there to catch it?
The needles or roots upon the ground?
The rocks and moonlight all around?
Or by chance a passing wind?
     But it's sooner
     Done than said:
A pine cone comes down, caught
By the vastness and naught
Of the whole mountain.

山中暑意七品

空山松子

一粒松子落下來
沒一點預告
該派誰去接它呢？
滿地的松針或松根？
滿坡的亂石或月色？
或是過路的風聲？
　　說時遲
　　那時快
一粒松子落下來
被整座空山接住

II. Dusk the Smuggler

How, indeed, does dusk the smuggler
Manage the crossing of the border?
And how does the black-clad clan of night
Cover him on the other side?
How, in moments of unguardedness,
Are amethyst, topaz, and amber
Sneaked across by the truckload?
Most dubious are the westward silhouettes
Of pines unshaved and unkempt,
And the countless backs of hunched hills
Up and down against the skies.
Closely I watch the flight of sunset
Without so much as a wink,
Like a sharp-sighted border guard,
And never a clue can I detect.

黃昏越境

究竟，黃昏那偷渡客
是怎麼越境的呢？
而黑衣幫的夜色
又怎麼接應的呢？
怎麼一個分神
滿天的紫水晶，赤瑪瑙，黃玉
就統統走了私呢？
最可疑的是朝西
那一排鬍子松的背影
和起起伏伏不定
再也數不清的山脊
我守著晚霞的逃逸
幾乎沒移過眼睛
銳利像緝私的邊警
卻怎麼也找不到一點破綻

III. A Lamp Taking Its Stand

What the night so thickly surrounds
Is but the shadows of the mountain.
What the mountain shadows surround
Is but such a little lamp.
But such a little lamp indeed,
With not a star for a support.
How can the heavy siege be broken?
Not tonight, it cannot be.
    And so be it:
Let giant night take possession
Of every corner in the dark,
That this lonely lamp may take
Possession of the heart of night.

一燈就位

夜色密密麻麻圍住的
不過是一層層的山影
山影深深邃邃圍住的
不過是這麼一盞燈
不過是一盞燈罷了
又不見星光來接應
這重圍怎能就突破
至少，今夜還不行
　　就這樣吧
讓夜之巨靈去占領
黑暗的每一個角落
只留下這一盞孤燈
把夜的心臟占領

IV. Listening to the Night

Inmost in the mountain and the night,
Where all things merge in a dream,
What is more benign to the ear
Than silence altogether clear?
Surely history, long and loud,
Can still spare such a moment
Out of incessant argument?
But what's happening to the wind, you ask.
Oh, the wind?　That's the faint, faint echo
That intermittently waits
Upon the transit of time.

深山聽夜

山深夜永
萬籟都渾然一夢
有什麼比徹底的靜
更加耐聽的呢？
再長，再忙的歷史
也總有這麼一刻
是無須爭辯的吧？
可是那風呢，你說
風嗎？那是時間在過境
引起的一點點，偶爾
一點點迴音

V. Deep As a Well the Night

Deep as a well the night:
Not even the length of my rope
Reaches a rippling sound.
Up the mossy wall
How the wormy stars crawl!
Yet never so much as halfway up
Before the mouth of the well cries
"The day breaks!"

夜深似井

夜深似井
盡我的繩長探下去
怎麼還不到水聲？
蠢蠢的星子群
沿著苔壁爬上來
好慢啊
只怕還不到半路
井口就一聲叫
天亮了！

VI. The Open Gate of Night

The so-called night is but a frontier castle,
The night reader its lonely host.
The lamplight comes softly flowing
Into a spellbinding moat.
And, leaning on the lace of battlement,
The lonely host is full of thought.
For tall stand the two gates of the fort:
The south gate closed upon the present,
The north gate open unto the past.
    Once across the moat,
The meandering courier road
Soon loses itself in the mist.

夜開北門

所謂夜，不過是邊陲的城堡
夜讀人是孤戍的堡主
一彎燈光流過來
便成美麗的護城河了
倚著雉堞的花邊
堡主是寂寞而多思的
孤高的堡門有兩扇
閉著的南門向現代
敞著的北門向古遠
　　一過對岸
驛道就蜿入了荒煙

VII. The Sleepless Dog

Often, after the last train,
In this wide world there only remain,
A mile or half a mile away,
Some dogs barking, two or three.
Only my lamp knows, at such moments,
This greying head by the light
Is no less a sleepless dog,
One that watches a different night
And barks at different shades.
Only it takes a greater distance
—A hundred years away, for instance,
To hear it right.

不寐之犬

往往，末班車過後
天地之大也不過剩下
一里半里路外
遠屋的犬吠，三聲兩聲
只有燈能體會
這時辰，燈下的白頭人
也是一頭無寐之犬
但守的是另一種夜
吠的，是另一種黑影
只要遠一點聽
—— 譬如在一百年外
就聽得清清楚楚

Tick Tick Tock

Tick tick tock.

Tock tock tick.

Give me a pair of clogs

And I'll awake my youthful days

With their clumsy little clops.

Up the lane,

Down the lane,

Tick tock tick,

Tock tick tock.

Tick tick tock.

Tock tock tick.

Give me a pair of clogs,

And old-time summer will recall me

To catch up with all those merry pals.

Up the lane,

Down the lane,

Tick tock tick,

Tock tick tock.

踢踢踏

踢踢踏
踏踏踢
給我一雙小木屐
讓我把童年敲敲醒
像用笨笨小樂器
　　從巷頭
　　到巷底
　　踢力踏拉
　　踏拉踢力

踢踢踏
踏踏踢
給我一雙小木屐
童年的夏天在叫我
去追趕別的小把戲
　　從巷頭
　　到巷底
　　踢力踏拉
　　踏拉踢力

Stamp and tramp.

Tramp and stamp.

Give me a pair of sandal wooden

And I'll join my girlish fair

And drag them all over the summer square

From sunrise

To sundown,

Tramp and stamp,

Stamp and tramp.

Tick tock tick.

Tock tick tock.

Give me a pair of clogs,

The magic rhythm would lead me back

To the coziness of legendry.

Up the lane,

Down the lane

Tick tock tick

Tock tick tuck

跺了蹬
　　蹬了跺
給我一雙小木拖
童年的夏天真熱鬧
成群的木柁滿地拖
　　從日起
　　到日落
　　跺了蹬蹬
　　蹬了跺跺

　　踢踢踏
　　踏踏踢
給我一隻小木屐
魔幻的節奏帶領我
走回童話的小天地
　　從巷頭
　　到巷底
　　踢力踏拉
　　踏拉踢力

201

The Spider Webs

Dusk is a sneaky spider
That steals across the water,
Trotting on its multiple legs,
Not a trace on the tranquil sea.
You never know where, for sure,
The landing is to be,
And find only too late,
At a surprised backward glance,
That we have all been captured
In the vastness of its webs.

蛛　網

暮色是一隻詭異的蜘蛛
躡水而來襲
複足暗暗地起落
平靜的海面卻不見蹤跡
也不知要向何處登陸
只知道一回顧
你我都已被擒
落進它吐不完的灰網裏去了

Once upon A Candle

The night when electricity failed,
A stub of candle offered to join me
On a homebound trip to a long-lost world.
Its manner in showing me the long way back
And the light it upheld in companionship
Were at once so familiar and kind
That I could not help suspecting
It was the very candle in my childhood
That, on a rainy night among Szechwan hills,
Had tended me reading until the threshold
Of dream, when it went out in a smoke.
Every candle stub with a heart of wick
Tells a tale with a tongue of flame.
Was the one the other night the very one
That had lighted me forty years ago?
"Are you really the one, candle?" I asked.
But a passing breeze left it wavering
Lightly, as if its answer were no,
And, then in ambiguity, as if yes.
Even though it had been the same old stub
And in my charmed gaze betrayed itself,

問　燭

偶然，在停電的晚上
一截白蠟燭有心伴我
去探久已失落的世界
看它殷勤帶路的姿勢
和眷眷照顧著我的清光
是那樣熟悉而可親
—— 不免令人懷疑
它就是小時候巴山夜雨
陪我念書到夢的邊緣
才黯然化煙而去的那枝
每一截蠟燭有一段故事
用蕊芯細細地訴給火聽
桌上的這一截真的就是
四十年前相望的那枝？
真的就是嗎，燭啊，我問你
一陣風過你輕輕地搖頭
有意無意地像在說否
無意有意地又像在說是
—— 就算你真是從前的那截
在恍然之間被我認出

How could I in my naivete expect
Its recognition, in this magic flicker,
Of me, a graying stranger through the years,
As the young head thick with dark hair?

又怎能指望，在搖幻的光中
你也認得出這就是我
認出眼前，哎，這陌生的白髮
就是當日烏絲的少年？

The Pearl Necklace

Long scattered in the recesses of memory,
The precious years that we had shared,
Never expected to be recovered,
Were displayed on a blue porcelain plate
By the salesgirl of the jewelry shop,
Who came up to us and, smiling, asked:
"Would this one, of eighteen inches, do?"
So thirty long years were strung in line:
Dear years, where a year spanned hardly an inch,
Where each pearl, silver and shimmering,
Warm and full, was calling back
A treasured day we spent together:
Each pearl a fine day dewdrop,
Or on a wet day a raindrop,
Or a bead in a rosary told
And retold on days each the other missed.
So the thread goes all the way

珍珠項鍊

滾散在回憶的每一個角落
半輩子多珍貴的日子
以為再也拾不攏來的了
卻被那珠寶店的女孩子
用一只藍磁的盤子
帶笑地托來我面前，問道
十八寸的這一條，合不合意？
就這麼，三十年的歲月成串了
一年還不到一寸，好貴的時光啊
每一粒都含著銀灰的晶瑩
溫潤而圓滿，就像有幸
跟你同享的每一個日子
每一粒，晴天的露珠
每一粒，陰天的雨珠
分手的日子，每一粒
牽掛在心頭的念珠
串成有始有終的這一條項鍊

Through the sun and the moon, around your neck,
And, in eighteen inches, through our double life.

—September 2, 1986
our 30th wedding anniversary

依依地靠在你心口
全憑這貫穿日月
十八寸長的一線因緣

　　　　　　　——September 2, 1986
　　　　　　　結婚三十週年紀念

The Swimmer

Let me with a headlong plunge O rolling sea,

Jump splashing into your tides.

A prostrate swimmer, I only mean

To turn myself to you, nothing held.

My only wish is for you, dearest nymph,

To grant me a safe passage across.

But why are the tides so restless tonight,

And, where, my patroness, are you carrying me,

A poor swimmer to cross?   The engulfing threat

Is tangled seaweeds on the whirls' edge,

The mermaid humming at my ear.

Were I a mariner I'd be seasick

With help of neither oar nor helm,

My sweating chest breathless in gasp.

Do you really mean to drown me, your pilgrim,

And deny me survival after all

The narrow straits and coral reefs?

O submerging tides endlessly coming,

泳　者

就讓我一縱而入吧，波動的海
縱入你迴盪的水域
一個匍拜的泳者，我不過
以身許海，更無保留
只求你，至愛的水神，保佑
順流平安地泅到對岸
但今晚的海流這般起伏
究竟要帶我，一個可憐的渡者
到哪裏去呢？　最誘人的危險
是海藻在漩渦的邊上盤旋
耳畔似傳來人魚的吟歌
若我是船夫怕也要暈船
何況此刻無舵又無槳
汗濕的胸膛喘息著無助
你真的要溺斃我嗎，你的信徒？
這險峽與珊瑚的暗礁
當真不讓人活著泅渡？
不斷湧來的一陣陣潮水啊

I'm on the edge of drowning, please!
Waft my sea-victim's nakedness
Lightly, to the calm of the sandy beach.

我快要力盡了，快要
請把這海難的赤體
送到平靜的沙灘上去吧
——輕，輕

What Is the Rain Saying through the Night?

What is the rain saying through the night?

The lamp upstairs asks

The tree by the window,

And the tree by the window asks

The car down the lane.

What is the rain saying through the night?

The car down the lane asks

The road to the horizon,

And the road to the horizon asks

The bridge up the stream.

What is the rain saying through the night?

The bridge up the stream asks

The umbrella of my boyhood,

And the umbrella of my boyhood asks

The shoes wet inside out.

What is the rain saying through the night?

The shoes wet inside out ask

The frogs croaking all around,

雨聲說些什麼

一夜的雨聲說些什麼呢？
樓上的燈問窗外的樹
窗外的樹問巷口的車
一夜的雨聲說些什麼呢？
巷口的車問遠方的路
遠方的路問上游的橋
一夜的雨聲說些什麼呢？
上游的橋問小時的傘
小時的傘問濕了的鞋
一夜的雨聲說些什麼呢？
濕了的鞋問亂叫的蛙

And the croaking frogs ask
The fog falling on all sides.
What is it saying, the rain, all night?
The falling fog asks
The lamp upstairs;
And the lamp upstairs asks
The man under the lamp;
And the man under the lamp
Looks up and asks:
    Why is it still raining
    From antiquity till tonight,
    From a drizzle to a downpour,
    From the eaves to the ocean shore?
I'm asking you, snail-slow moss,
What is the rain saying through the night?

亂叫的蛙問四周的霧
說些什麼呢，一夜的雨聲？
四周的霧問樓上的燈
樓上的燈問燈下的人
燈下的人抬起頭來說
　　怎麼還沒有停啊：
　　從傳說落到了現在
　　從霏霏落到了湃湃
　　從簷漏落到了江海
問你啊，蠢蠢的青苔
一夜的雨聲說些什麼呢？

Scenes of Kengting National Park

I. Tachienshan

Always, a look upward finds you on high,
A look backward finds you against the sky.
Of all scenes Kengting Park is the last word,
And you are the last word of the park.
Spring may try her hardest to climb
Without hope of reaching your waist.
Howling winds and straying clouds
Are forced to detour for your sake.
A rock tower of such manly state
Deserves to be lifted by all eyes
To the very skies.

墾丁十一首

大尖山

抬頭，你永遠在上面
回頭，你永遠在天邊
墾丁是一切風景的結論
而你是墾丁的焦點
無論春天如何攀爬
都不能抵達你的半腰
天風和野雲都為你改道
陽剛之美的一座石塔
所有仰望的眼光合力
將你供舉到天際

II. Noonday Slumber of a Faun

"Is the faun at home?" lightly I ask.
A long pause without an answer.
Nothing but cool breeze and chirping birds,
And impenetrable remains the wood.
"Is the faun at home?" again I ask.
And again silence is the response.
So the bulldozer's impending arm
Will not knock on your door today,
Where dense and dark the foliage droops.
Nor will loudspeakers and traffic
Break in upon your profound sleep.
Listen, nothing but silence.

牧神午寐

牧神在家嗎？　我輕輕問道
半天，都沒有人回答
除了清涼的風聲，脆利的禽語
似乎探不到森林的底細
牧神在家嗎？　又問了一遍
應我依然是一片靜寂
至少，挖土機無禮的長臂
今天還不會就來叫門
背光的濃蔭低垂著翠影
也沒有擴音機和馬達
來驚動你深沉的午寐
聽哪，真的是沒有

III. Wind-Sheared Tree

Not even the fiercest winds can tear up
The green life of this half tree,
A half-mast flag never lowered.
Half of the roots propped in the air,
The other half, even stronger of will,
Fast braced against the rock,
Wrestle with wind after bullying wind
And sooner will break up than kneel.
And so, with a tingling frame,
It takes its stand right in the mouth
Of all that howl and hoot in space.

風翦樹

再強悍的風季也休想拔起
這半樹青翠的生機
永不下降的一面半旗
一半的頑根撐在空際
另一半，更頑固的意志
緊緊踹住最後的岩石
和欺人的風勢一較摔跤
拚著腰斷，也不甘跪倒
就這麼一身錚錚的傲骨
翹在咆哮呼喝的風口
都來吧，天上的狂飆

IV. The Golden Hour

Dear is the magic golden hour
When slant is light and oblique
Stretch all the shadows.
A vastness of incredible splendor
Needle after needle skillfully knit
With sunset's threads of fine silk.
If you could find where all began
And lightly draw and quietly pull,
You surely could catch
All these red-gold scales in one net.

金色時辰

最可惜是這奇幻的時辰
光是斜光，影是側影
一整幅不可能的絢豔
用落日的細絲線
一針針密密地鉤成
只要你能夠找到線頭
輕輕地抽，靜靜地收
就能夠把這滿海的赤金鱗
一網都打盡

V. Toilers on the Sea

Is the sunset splendor burning orange-red
Someone's far, far-off cry,
A cry for you with echoes across the sky?
Time for supper now, toilers on the sea,
How can you, over the rolling waste,
Find your fair-wind homeward way?
How can your boat with breast brave
The plash and dash, wave after wave,
And out of the depth of Kuroshiu current
Pull up nets of bouncing catch?
When net is heavy and catch is plenty,
Well for the full hold, well for you.
When net is light, O well for those
Poor survivors, well for the fish.

討海人

天一樣長的霞火燒著橘色
是遠方有人在喊你
在遠方喊你的回聲嗎？
晚飯的時候了，討海人
荒涼而顛簸的水路，何處
才是你順風的回程？
一條小漁船的胸脯
要承受滿海滾滾的浪頭
向黑潮的深處去索討
一網又一網的生鮮活跳
──若是網重而魚多
滿艙的豐收該慶賀，為你
若是網輕呢，唉，也該慶幸
又逃過了一劫，為魚

VI. Sandspits of Paoli Brook

Clear fresh waters from Payao Hill
Come winding downhill and singing
A babbling carefree pastoral song
To join the saltiness of the straits.
The stretch of blue is already in sight
And within earshot is the tide,
When the narrow sandspits bar the way,
Saying, "No exit now winter's here."
So wait on, stranded little boats,
Until summer has fully fed the brook
With upstream rain and the new flood
Dashes wide open winter's ban.
And one by one a song of freedom
Shall spit you forth onto the sea.

保力溪砂嘴

八瑤山下清清的淡水
左轉右迴，一路下坡
哼著一首無愁的牧歌
來赴海峽鹹鹹的約會
已經望見那一片水藍
聽見海潮一陣陣在呼喊
卻被砂洲的手臂攔住
說冬天到了，不准出海去
等吧，擱淺的小木船
等夏天把河谷灌得肥滿
上游的雨水奔瀉而來
把冬之禁令一下子衝開
唱一首自由之歌，把你們
一一，吐給大海

VII. Shell's Sand

The white sand beach is a sea-land exchange.
Look at Poseidon's booth, so rich
With exquisite corals and shells,
Ground by wind and wave from time antique,
Rubbed slow and fine by tiny sand, and washed
Into tints that charm whoever looks.
Whose box is it, nymph, that squanders
So many, many gifts on us?
And what could man offer in exchange
Except such holiday trash
As empty beer bottles and broken cigarette packs?

貝殼砂

白淨的沙灘是水陸的交易會
你來看，海神的攤位
多精巧的珊瑚與貝殼
不計歲月的琢磨，被風，被浪
被細緻的沙粒慢揉又細搓
洗出人寵人愛的光澤
是從哪位水精的寶盒
滾翻出來的這許多珍品
就這麼大方，海啊，都送給了我們
而人呢，拿什麼跟她交換？
除了一地的假期垃圾
破香菸盒子和空啤酒罐

VIII. Mountain-Sea Falls

With a shout you push the sky and cliff aside
In so peremptory a way
And let a profusion of limpidity,
Foaming and spurting, in a wild jump
Come falling down with a deadening din.
No hill or valley can ever stop,
No rock under the cliff can scare,
Nothing whatever can restrain
The undaunted will in quest of exit,
For waiting outside there for you
Is no other than the sea.

山海瀑

一聲大喝，推開長空與高崖
以如此斷然的姿態
奔放而充沛的清白
就從最高處，瀉沫飛珠
在轟轟的呼駭裏一縱而來
萬壑千山都攔你不住
崖下的怪石也不能嚇阻
誰都擋不了一條活水
向絕路尋找自己的生路
只因在山外把你等待的
不是別人，是海

IX. The Frog Rock

Down there, the sea has been calling you
For thousands and thousands of years.
Why are you still squatting on the beach?
How did you come jumping here,
And where, where were you going
When you came to such a sudden stop
As if seized with a binding spell?
Wake up, dark green giant monster,
And break the fetters of overgrown moss.
Tonight, with fair moonlight on the bay,
Carry me on your back and jump
Over the small pond of the sea,
Hopping from isle to fairy isle.

青蛙石

在腳下喊你好幾千年了，那海
怎麼你還是蹲在岸邊？
你如何跳來的呢，當初
正預備要跳去何處？
卻突然就這麼楞住了
像中了，咳，誰的法術
醒一醒吧，墨綠的巨靈
掙開青苔密密的羅網
趁今夜，南灣的月色正好
讓我騎上你背脊，跳吧
把大海跳成小池塘
從一座仙島到一座仙島

X. The Gray-Faced Buzzard

Long are the winds, blowing down all those latitudes,
That carry this guest from distant lands,
With wings weathered by Mongolian storms
And associations of northern tales.
Miles upon miles over the clouds,
Through vast autumn you have come.
May you be greeted, not by the hunter,
But by the palatable lizard and snake
And the freedom of our southern sky,
That you may take home the warm thought:
"I've been to a lovely island."

灰面鵟

高高的緯度啊長長的風
吹來一個遠遠的過客
兩翼還帶著塞外的風霜
和江湖傳說的聯想
無邊的秋色攔你不住
雲程迢迢是幾千里路呢？
但願迎你的是美味的蜥蜴
是蛇，是昆蟲，不是獵者
是南方自由的晴空，只為讓你
帶著溫暖的記憶回去
「我到過一個，哦，可愛的島嶼」

XI. The Black-Spotted Butterfly

Is there Heaven in every wild flower?
How many Heavens, then, will be enough?
How free is the Apostle of Beauty
That hovers in a white-cape dance!
Into this life once hard you crawled,
And out of it, lightly, you should fly.
Then fly away while spring is young,
Away to the philosopher's dream.
Yet beware of the entomologist
Or you stumble into his net
And, pierced by a ruthless pin,
Look vivid in mockery of life.

大白斑蝶

一朵花真的是一個天國嗎？
要探多少個天國才滿足呢？
多自由啊，唯美的使徒
這麼翩翩地素妝而舞
這世界，你辛苦地爬來
就應該瀟灑地飛去
乘春天還年輕，飛吧
飛回哲學家正甜的午夢
一路要提防，切莫闖進
昆蟲學家採標本的袋網
讓一根無情的針
穿腸成唯美的栩栩如生

後記：小品十九首自七十五年底至七十六年初陸續寫成，均為題
　　　王慶華的攝影而作，並與張曉風、鍾玲、羅青、席慕蓉、
　　　林清玄、蔣勳等同類小品收入七十六年八月出版的《墾丁
　　　國家公園詩文攝影集》。此為其中的十一品。

Dream and Bladder

Whether it's a luring wet dream
Or a raving nightmare,
Whether you dream of turning
Into a bear or a bug
Or into a hovering butterfly,
Whether your soul soars to the stars
Or swims on its back in the moonlight,
It takes only four hundred c. c.
To apply just a little pressure
Upon the balloon of your bladder
To call you back from afar
On your pilgrimage to heavan
Or your banishment to hell.
All these, to a sprinkling tune,
Are to spatter and scatter away
Half in drowsiness before daybreak.

夢與膀胱

無論是綺夢而迷
或者是惡夢而囈
無論是夢見了熊
或是夢變了甲蟲
或者是夢蝶而栩栩
當靈魂升向星際
或是在月光裏仰泳
只要有四百西西
向膨脹的膀胱
施這麼一點壓力
就把你遠召了回來
無論是天國之行
或者是地獄之旅
都在破曉前的惺忪裏
隨著水聲淙淙
一瀉而去

The Gecko

You solitary hunter, clad all in gray,
Climbing the vertical as if on the level.
Did you teach the transcendent skill
Of scaling the wall, of belly-swimming,
Of hanging upside down from the ceiling?
What is dizziness, you ask, what
Is really meant by slope or steep?
The night of sheer ascent hinders not
Your dash improbable, to and fro,
Your tapering tail brushing by.
Neither flies nor mosquitoes can
Escape your long tongue's sudden dart.
How many midnights am I indebted
To your silent fellowship when,
Looking up, I saw you watch from on high?
Whose palace, my sleepless guard, do you watch?
This austere study of mine is
No palace of art or ivory tower,
And like you I'm also a hunter used
To lone expedition, but never learned
Your knack of capturing with one leap.

壁　虎

獨行的灰衣客，履險如夷
走壁的輕功是你傳授的嗎？
貼游的步法，倒掛的絕技
什麼是懼高症呢，你問
什麼是陡峭，什麼是傾斜？
仰面矗起的長夜
任你竄去又縱來
細尾倏忽在半空搖擺
蚊蠅和蜘蛛都難逃
你長舌一吐，猝到的飛鏢
多少深夜感謝你伴陪
一抬頭總見你在上面相窺
是為誰守宮呢，不眠的禁衛？
這苦練的書房並非
藝術之宮或象牙之塔
跟你一樣我也是獵戶
也慣於獨征，卻尚未練成
一撲就成擒的神技，像你

Your smooth highway is my fatal pass,
But that is no objection why lonely host
And lonely guest should not ever meet
Virtually in vertical communion.
Though you're born a tiger and I a dragon,
Though snatching a fly you roar a tiger-roar,
And catching a happy phrase I would
Chant in my long-drawn dragon mood,
The dragon need not fight the tiger.
And, now prostrate on the windowpane,
With the starry night on your back,
The nakedness of your tiny life,
Translucent with miniature entrails,
Is all unguarded and fully under
The piercing glare of my reading lamp.
If you enjoy this simple story
I've written for your life, do tell me—
"Chit-chat-chit!"

你的坦途是我的險路
卻不妨寂寞相對的主客
結為垂直相交的伴侶
雖然你屬虎而我屬龍
你捕蠅而虎嘯，我獲句而龍吟
龍吟虎嘯未必要鬥爭
此刻，你攀伏在窗玻璃外
背著一夜的星斗，五臟都透明
小小的生命坦然裸裎
在炯炯的燈下，全無戒心
讓我為你寫一篇小傳
若是你會意，就應我一聲吧！
——唧唧

The Sunflowers

—on a painting by van Gogh

The mallet raised in Christie's room,

    Going,

    Going,

    Gone,

Comes thumping down.

So with thirty-nine million are bought

The tightened breaths in the room

And the bulging eyes over the world.

Yet forever beyond ransom

Is the ear that was sliced,

The red hair that was scorched,

The decayed teeth that went loose.

Forever sold are the thirty-seven years.

The mallet is raised at the excited crowd,

The pistol was raised at the lonely heart —

    Going, the sliced ear,

    Going, the scorched hair,

    Going, the decayed teeth,

    Going, the haunted dreams,

    Going, the fits of convulsions,

向日葵

木槌在克莉絲蒂的大廳上
    going
    going
    gone
砰然的一響，敲下去
三千九百萬元的高價
買斷了，全場緊張的呼吸
買斷了，全世界驚羨的眼睛
買不回，斷了，一隻耳朵
買不回，焦了，一頭赤髮
買不回，鬆了，一嘴壞牙
買不回匆匆的三十七歲
木槌舉起，對著熱烈的會場
手槍舉起，對著寂寞的心臟
    斷耳，going
    赤髮，going
    壞牙，going
    惡夢，going
    羊癲瘋，going

Going, the letters and the diary,
Going, the doctors and the sickbeds,
Going, Dear Theo my brother—
And with a bang all, all was gone,
When the generous heart
Burst into sunflowers and flowering suns.

　　　　日記和信，going
　　　　醫師和病床，going
　　　　親愛的弟弟啊，going
砰然的一響，gone
一顆慷慨的心臟
迸成滿地的向日葵滿天的太陽

後記：一九八七年三月三十日，梵谷誕辰三十四週年，他的一幅
　　　向日葵在倫敦克莉絲蒂拍賣公司賣出，破紀錄的高價是美
　　　金三千九百八十五萬元。Going, going, gone是拍賣成交時
　　　的吆喝，語終而木槌敲下。

The Diver

With a deep breath taking the challenge of space,
The moment before departure he stares into blankness
And with the void below designs
How his brief busy trip,
Unimpeded and precise,
Should, during the headlong fall,
Penetrate the trinity
Of dynamics, aesthetics, aeronautics.
For the freedom of three seconds only
It took him three years' hard exercise
To turn discipline into instinct
Against the powerful pull of tyrant earth.
His back turned on the waters below,
Standing on the very edge of land
With tiptoe hold, he raises both arms.
Look at the perfection of his muscles,
Silhouetted contour against the sky,
By the flapping of ripples and winds
Stream-line polished into suppleness
And branded by the basking sun
With the mellowness of copper tone.

跳水者

深呼吸向他挑戰的空間
出發前一剎那他定下眼神
向下面的虛無設計
他緊湊的短程應該
用怎樣的姿態，精確而流利
在降落的途中一穿而過
力學，美學，和飛的奇蹟
三秒鐘的自由罷了
歷經三年的苦練，把自律
練成了本能，只為抗衡
大地引力威武的命令
背著下面的水世界
他棲止在陸地的邊緣
踮著腳尖，高高地舉起雙臂
從趾尖到指尖，看他的肌腱
完美的輪廓反托著天空
久被拍胸的浪迎面的風
磨成勃然起伏的流線
更讓太陽把皮膚烘烤
熟成古銅色調的烙印

So to the limit he stretches himself
For the suddenness of a fall and roll
Into a quick succession of somersaults
As a worship ritual to the sea nymph.
And just before touching the water
He straightens up into an arrow
And finds himself right on time,
With joined hands, palm to palm,
To break open with a crisp plop,
The flashing glass of a revolving door
And disappears behind, leaving only
The trickle of a momentary splash
As a signature of his transit.

他把自己引伸到極限
就倏地一落又一捲
捲入一連串的天翻地覆
翻成一連串拜海的觔斗
而在要觸到水面之前
又倏地拉直成一枝箭
恰恰趕得及用合掌
　清脆的一聲響
撞開閃亮的玻璃門
便沒入了門裏，只留下
一灑急濺的浪花，
當作他過境的簽名

Mother, I'm Hungry

Mother, I'm hungry,
But I can't swallow.
Such a bitter taste
Chokes my throat all day long:
How can I swallow?

Mother, I'm tired,
But I can't sleep.
Such a heavy feeling
Pounds my chest all night long:
How can I sleep?

Mother, I'm dead,
But I'm not resigned.
Such a tortured country
Brands my soul forever:
How can I give up?

Mother, I'm gone.
On Tomb-Sweeping Day

媽媽，我餓了

媽媽，我餓了
但是我吃不下
這麼苦的滋味
整天哽在我喉頭
我怎麼吞得下？

媽媽，我累了
但是我睡不著
這麼重的感覺
整夜壓在我胸口
我怎麼睡得著？

媽媽，我死了
但是我不瞑目
這麼慘的國家
永遠烙在我魂魄
我怎麼放得下？

媽媽，我走了
明年的清明節

Come back to recall my soul

In democratic years,

In Tiananmen Square.

記得來為我招魂
在民主的歲月
在這天安門下

In Praise of Hong Kong

Just as that brave young man,
The noblest and most favored
Of all the children
Of Goddess of Democracy,
By the unbending of his spine
And the openness of his breast
Stopped the stamping tanks,
A whole clattering fleet of them,
And turned them all at once
Into confounded crabs
On the fatal street of June,

You are such a hero
To stand all by yourself
And face bigger tanks
Clanking with heavier treads,
Louder in your protest,
And, while the world watches by
Single-handed you resist,
Crushing down upon you,
The tank fleet of the years:

讚香港

正如那年輕的勇士
潔白的民主女神
最心愛最高貴的孩子
憑一根脊椎的挺直
和一面胸膛的擔當
就把一整列輾來的坦克
像無頭的螃蟹
統統阻擋
在六月的大街上

你也是那樣的一位
敢於獨立的豪傑
敢在更大的坦克之前
仰對更重噸的威脅
發出響亮的怒吼
在世界的旁觀下
只有你獨臂抵擋
歲月的坦克隊當頂輾來

1990,
1991,
1992,
1993,
1994...
until at last
comes all too fast
1997.

一九九〇
一九九一
一九九二
一九九三
一九九四
直到最後
來得太快的
一九九七

The Langlois Bridge

—on a painting by van Gogh

A clanking drawbridge with rattling chains,
Connecting both banks of the canal:
Was this where once you trudged across
To a gas lamp, sooty and yellow,
To meet the family of potato-eaters
Hunched all around a greasy table?
Did you really cross the bridge
To the women who grudged you love,
To pits even deeper and damper than hell,
To Rachel's scream and Gauguin's scorn,
Flashing a razor in your hand,
To the asylum's endless corridor
Beyond the sanity of common men,
To Lamartine Square's scorching heat,
The loneliness of roadside café
And the lonelier haloes of moon and stars,
To the golden fields when July came on,

荷蘭吊橋

—— 梵谷百年祭

一座鏗鏘的吊橋，纜索轆轆
連接小運河的兩岸，當初
你就是從此地過河
走向一盞昏黃的油燈
去找圍坐著一張小桌子
吃馬鈴薯的那一家農人嗎？
你真的這麼走過橋去
走向不能愛你的女人
走向深於地獄的礦坑
走向娜莎的驚呼，高敢的冷笑
手裏亮著帶血的剃刀
走向瘋人院深邃的長廊
向回不了頭的另一世界
走向悶熱的拉馬丁廣場
走向寂寞的露天酒座
和更加寂寞的星光，月光
七月來時，走向田野的金黃

The swooping crows and the surging corn?
Yet what you lifted to the sun
Was not a brush but a gun.

The bang that hadn't startled the world

Till after a century the echo came
Bringing five million across the bridge
To flood hotels, restaurants, museums
And jostle in long waiting lines to see
What none but your brother
Had cared to turn and glance:
      The sunflowers,
      The irises,
      The starry night,
      The whole splendor of a new world.

向騷動的鴉群，洶湧的麥浪
為何你舉起的一把
不是畫筆，是手槍？

那一響並沒有驚醒世界

要等一百年才傳來回聲
於是五百萬人都擠過橋去
去擠滿旅館，餐館，美術館
去蠕蠕的隊伍裏探頭爭看
看當初除了你弟弟
沒有人肯跟你
過橋去看一眼的
　　　向日葵
　　　鳶尾花
　　　星光夜
那整個耀眼的新世界

By the Darkening Window

By the darkening window I'm writing a poem
Which by nightfall I must finish
Or else I could not sleep at ease.
For dusk has been lurking all around
And is now gathering to engulf
Brilliant evening clouds one by one.
The dubious window is under threat
And snow-white paper may not hold,
As a besieged fortress, so rumor says,
Is about to give up to the foe.
Many a time the desk lamp has hinted
That I could beckon for its help,
But I refused saying this encounter
Must be settled between me and night
With none else to upset the rules.
Just as daylight is denied by darkness,
Night will be refuted by the stars,
But that is to be judged on high
And to be dreamed of during the sleep.
Meanwhile, the gray presence is on the page,
Menacing the title and subtitle

在漸暗的窗口

在漸暗的窗口趕寫一首詩
天黑以前必須要完成
否則入睡的時候不甘心
只因暮色潛伏在四野
越集越密，吞併了晚霞
曖昧的窗口已受到威脅
雪淨的稿紙恐將不守
像謠傳即將放棄的孤城
桌燈在一旁幾度示意
只等我招手，願來救急
卻被我拒絕了，說，這場對決
是我跟夜晚之間的競賽
不容第三者來攪亂規則
正如白晝被黑暗否定
黑暗也被否定於繁星
不過那將是高處的判決
入睡以後或者會夢見
說著，灰靄已逼到紙角
陰影正伸向標題，副標題

And leaving the pen alone holding its ground
And struggling amidst the tightening siege,
Still convinced of its final freedom.
So for my peace on pillow before sleep
Am I rescuing by the darkening window
The poem to be finished before night falls.

只剩下筆尖還不肯放棄
還在重圍的深處奔突
相信最後會破陣而出
只為了入睡前能夠安枕
要乘天未黑透就完成
在快暗的窗口搶救的詩

Holding My Grandson

Pillowed upon my arm, the lightness of ten pounds;
Nestled against my chest, the shortness of two feet.
Even without reincarnation have I the feeling
Of a second life, remembering how,
Thirty-five years ago, on that island,
In just the same gesture I held and lulled
Another baby, your mother. Though the scene
Outside the window now is snowy New York,
In my lap I seem to hold that same dear child.
Mewling as its mother once did, toothless,
Nebulous yet in its first innocence,
And neither blinking nor looking away,
It gazes on me with such intent eyes,
Pure as a pair of dark crystal balls.
Sheer inexperience has yet to learn
How to return my smile with a smile.
So across the generations in amazement,
You look up at history where worldliness
Has turned to page sixty-five.
When, indeed, can you read it from the title page?

抱　孫

十磅之輕，仰枕在我的臂彎
兩尺之短，蜷靠在我的胸膛
不待輪迴，已恍然隔世
三十五年前，在那島上
也曾經如此抱著，搖著
另一個孩子，你的母親
只換了，窗外，是紐約的雪景
卻幻覺，懷裏，是從前的稚嬰
同樣是乳臭咻咻，乳齒未萌
渾然的天真尚未揭曉
專注的眼神不眨也不移
這麼出神地將我打量
清澈澈一雙黑水晶體
純粹的稚氣一時還不懂
用笑容來回應我的笑容
就這麼驚異地隔代相望
你仰望著歷史，看滄桑
已接近封底，掀到了六十五頁
幾時，你才會從頭讀起呢？

How many chapters, no, how many passages

Can your mother tell you when you are grown?

And down at future I look, at the riddle

Yet to be solved, the story yet to unfold,

Wondering what a century the twenty-first will be,

Reflected on these pupils, the tiny twin

Where changing and chasing images go.

Too young to be a prophecy are you;

Too old not to be an allusion am I.

How could the end of experience ever meet

The start of innocence, just through the first month,

Unless by hugging you all to myself,

Most primitive, by bodily press and heat,

By blood upstream calling blood downstream,

The way years and, oh, years ago,

In the old house in that island town

With an alley echoing cicadas

And a window leafy with green twilight,

I held and lulled

And lulled and held

Another new-born child, your mother?

當你長大，從母親的口裏
會聽到其中的幾章，幾節？
我俯窺著未來，看謎面
天機未動，故事正等待破題
一對小巧的瞳人，滴溜圓滾
幻象和倒影所由孿生
要轉向怎樣的廿一世紀？
你太小了，還不算是預言
我太老了，快變成了典故
世故的盡頭如何接通
天真的起點呢，剛剛滿月
除非是貼身將你抱住
最最原始，用體溫，用觸覺
用上游的血喊下游的血
宛如從前，在島城的古屋
一巷蟬聲，半窗樹影
就這麼抱著，搖著
　　　　搖著，抱著
另一個初胎的嬰孩，你母親

On Such a Windy Night

On such a windy night,
When a window there is
That hasn't closed up,
Whose ear is it
That hasn't closed up yet?

On such a windy night,
When a star there is
That hasn't blown out,
Whose eye is it
That hasn't blown out yet?

On such a windy night,
When a flag there is
That hasn't furled up,
Whose soul is it
That hasn't furled up yet?

I close the window,
Take down the flag,
And blow out the star

在多風的夜晚

在多風的夜晚
有一扇窗子
還沒有關閉
是誰的耳朵呢
還不關閉

在多風的夜晚
有一盞星子
還沒有休息
是誰的眼睛呢
還不休息

在多風的夜晚
有一面旗子
還沒有收起
是誰的靈魂呢
還不收起

我向天邊
吹熄了星子
收下旗子

In the far sky,
Yet still I find

An ear there is
That hasn't closed yet;
Whose window is it,
On such a windy night,
That cannot close?

An eye there is
That hasn't blown out yet;
Whose star is it,
On such a windy night,
That cannot blow out?

A soul there is
That hasn't furled up yet;
Whose flag is it
That cannot furl up
On such a windy night?

關上窗子
卻仍然發現

有一扇耳朵
還沒有關閉
誰的窗子
在多風的夜晚
不能關閉

有一盞眼睛
還沒有休息
誰的星子
在多風的夜晚
不能休息

有一面靈魂
還沒有收起
誰的旗子
在多風的夜晚
不能收起

No Lullaby

Setting the straits all astir,
Why is the wind tonight
So full of anxieties?
Will the distraught sleeper spend
A long night of bad dreams
Or one of sleeplessness?
I seem to ask myself
Or, in the face of the void,
Ask the nearly spent age.
As long is the wind over the sea,
So long is the night here upstairs.
Rather than thus sit up alone
Throughout such a windy night
While the soul-recalling blast
Through the cracks of childhood
Sweeps across the straits, screaming
With frightful echoes of the past,
I would fret in fitful sleep,
Though troubled by nightmares stalking,
When left shoulder and right in turn
Must take the pressure on the side

非安眠曲

令整個海峽都不安
今晚這風聲何以
充滿了預感和回憶
而今晚的睡眠
會夜長而夢多嗎
或是更深而無寐
我像是在問自己
又像是對著蒼茫
在問將盡的世紀
海上的風有多長
樓上的夜就多長
與其無寐而聽風
聽隱隱喊魂的風聲
穿透童年的裂縫
呼嘯過海峽而來
帶著歷史的騷響
寧可輾轉而多夢
儘管惡魘會連連
儘管左肩換右肩
要擔負側身的壓力

Or my back or belly must bear
Strain from earth or from air
Or the long accumulation
Of layers of subtle inner wounds
Deep hid, conscious or unconscious.
Yet all these can simply be reduced
To only a muffled cry in dream
And a few turns to left and right
That turn at last to a dull gray dawn
Outside the window, peeping in.

不然脊椎或肋骨
要承受仰天或伏地
承受意識或潛意識
層層內傷的累積
也不過是一句夢囈
和恍惚幾次翻身
就渾然把窗外
暗昧的魚肚子翻白

All Throughout This My Life: To Mother

All throughout this my life
Twice in abandon did I cry.
Once, when my life began;
The other, when yours ended.
The first time, I couldn't remember but heard from you.
The second, you wouldn't know even if I told.
Yet all between these two cries
Long our laughter kept ringing
Again and again and again,
Ringing for fully thirty years.
This surely you did know
And surely I can't forget.

今生今世
——母難日之一

今生今世
我最忘情的哭聲有兩次
一次，在我生命的開始
一次，在你生命的告終
第一次，我不會記得，是聽你說的
第二次，你不會曉得，我說也沒用
但兩次哭聲的中間啊
有無窮無盡的笑聲
一遍一遍又一遍
迴盪了整整三十年
你，都曉得，我，都記得

Happy Was the World: To Mother

Happy was the world
Where, when first we met,
You greeted me with a smile,
And I answered with a cry
That moved heaven and earth.

Sad was the world
Where, when at last we parted,
I saw you off with a cry,
And you answered with a silence
That closed heaven and earth.

Strange was the world
Where, seeing you first or last,
I always cried aloud
How with your smile the world began
And how without it bliss ended.

矛盾世界
—— 母難日之二

快樂的世界啊
當初我們見面
你迎我以微笑
而我答你以大哭
驚天，動地

悲哀的世界啊
最後我們分手
我送你以大哭
而你答我以無言
關天，閉地

矛盾的世界啊
不論初見或永別
我總是對你大哭
哭世界始於你一笑
而幸福終於你閉目

The Flying Sunflower

—To Comet Hale-Bopp

Dalai Lama came and went with the rain.

For three days a strong wind blew, howling

And sweeping the sky clear of clouds, when in

You burst, a stranger from outer space

Beyond Tibet, more puzzling than its creed.

There you are, the stir of the western sky,

The focus of all the lenses busy adjusting,

When telescopes and binoculars are yelling,

Telling your arrival after an exile,

A long one, of more than forty centuries.

You flying sunflower, mother-possessed,

Are coming back to your dazzling home,

Your comet-coma trailing light blue hair

Combed by the fingers of solar wind

All across the space for millions of miles.

Your last appearance struck my naive sires

Speechless, dropping their bronze vessels in awe,

Upset, after the ominous eclipses,

By yet one more spectacle on high.

Your headlong intrusions and escapes broke

飛行的向日葵
——致海爾·鮑普彗星

達賴把雨季帶來了又帶去
一連三日，颳起呼嘯的勁風
掃淨濁霧，闢開空闊的青穹
赫然你來了，天外的遠客
比西藏更敻遠，密宗更神奇
你來了，西北的星空頓然轟動
所有的鏡頭都忙著調焦
所有單筒與雙筒，都在驚叫
說，你來了，失蹤的浪子
久放的流犯，一去四千二百年
一朵向日葵戀母成病
轉身尋你光燦的故鄉
回頭的彗星青髮飛揚
被撫於太陽風炎炎的火掌
橫空一億里曳著孺慕
上次你來時，我渺茫的先祖
放下青銅爵愕然仰望
刺眼的異象令人不解
日蝕，月蝕已經夠反常
何況你無端地闖進闖出

The seasonal order and left helpless

The Eight Diagrams and the Five Elements.

Did you really print your image upon

The double pupil of Patriarch Hsun,

Mirror it on the flood of Noah and Yu,

And glimpse the myths of Kung Kung and Kua Fu?

How can I ever sum up what has been

In your absence of four thousand years?

Most of the myths and faiths, when last you called,

Were yet unborn, history never known.

Ch'u Yuan and Homer, Confucius and Jesus,

Siddhartha Gautama and Socrates,

What a roll-call, happened only after you left.

My confused ancestors blamed all disasters

On your presence and in your weird light read

Flood and famine, war and changing dynasties.

Why of all seasons do you come back

In the unseemly hour of total eclipse

To a mother behind a black veil, leaving

Domestic feud known on all the front pages?

Yet in truth a dirty snow-ball you are,

Made a momentary superstar

By the doting glances of the smiling sun,

Your streaming locks but an outburst of dust.

Exiled by Jupiter to an icy prison

亂了曆書濛鴻的節氣
八卦，五行都安頓不了
你當真映過舜目重瞳
掠過夏禹和諾亞的洪波
見證過夸父和共工的故事
一去無消息悠悠四千載
漫長的前文該如何提要呢
神話與宗教，上次你來時
多半還沒有誕生，何況是歷史
屈原與荷馬，孔子與耶穌
蘇格拉底與釋迦牟尼
夜長夢多，全是你走後的事
我惶駭的祖先把天災，人禍
全怪在你頭上，不，在你彗尾
改朝，換姓，兵燹，凶年
都怪你出現得不對
為什麼這次你歸來，偏偏
要挑上日全蝕不祥的時辰
來投奔戴黑面紗的母親
把家變演上全世界的頭條
其實你原是雪球，一團邋遢
因太陽照顧而揚名星際
把微塵噴成唯美的飄髮
木星貶你做冰囚，拋你

On the very edge of the universe,

You are called back by the magnanimous sun.

You and I, casual travelers across the void,

Meet overnight in the Sahara

Of vacuum space to warm our hands

At the solar fire, where you comb your hair,

How magnificently, against the endless wind

And I turn and strike my verse hot in the fire.

Between my seventy years and your thousands

We share this unforgettable night

But must part company as soon as we meet.

"Good night" is all I'm left to say

To your kindly "until we meet again!"

 But at the dawn of creation who was it

That made this solar fire? How longer, then,

Could it burn on, and by whose care?   But who

Am I and who, my friend from way out there,

Are you? So across the starry wilderness,

That sends no echoes back, I ask

    The Hunter and the Wolf,

The Dipper and the spanning Milky Way.

                    —1997

去荒寒的邊境，幸有太陽
迢迢地將你召回母鄉
你我原都是宇宙的過客
在真空的戈壁偶然過夜，就著
太陽的風火爐烘手取暖
你逆風刷髮，我探火煉詩
我以七十歲為一夜，你以四千年
今夕才一見就要告別
我只能說晚安了，你還可說再見
而這風火爐，當初，開天闢地
是誰造的呢　還能燒多久
該誰來負責？而我又是誰呢，終究
不休的太空客啊，而你，又是誰？
向無壁回音的星墟啊我仰問
獵戶與天狼，北斗燦燦與河漢耿耿

　　　　　　　　　　──1997

On My Seventieth Birthday

Even the longest river shall meet the sea.
Ho much waterway is still left ahead
Before the exit delta greets me?
Surely the gorges have long been passed
And range after range has failed
To stop or stem the torrential flow.
Unhurried now are the lower reaches,
Joined by tributaries from afar.
Settled are the sands of the years.
Deep in tranquil night, listen
To the tidal sighs faint from the sea,
And melting snow back at the source
Starting in a trickle its expedition.
Even the longest river is bound for sea:
The water hurries on, the river stays.

七十自喻

再長的江河終必要入海
河口那片三角洲
還要奔波多久才抵達？
只知道早就出了峽
回望一道道橫斷山脈
關之不斷，阻之不絕
到此平緩已經是下游
多少支流一路來投奔
沙泥與歲月都已沉澱
寧靜的深夜，你聽
河口隱隱傳來海嘯
而河源雪水初融
正滴成清細的涓涓
再長的江河終必要入海
河水不回頭，而河長在

At the Twilight Hour

Mild evening, graceful evening,
When all the eyes are turning west
Where sunset, before his sea-burial
Under a sky of crimson splendor,
Says good-bye to this our old world
Like a tenor trailing his last aria.
Not even the dike, now, with all its length,
Can retain the shimmer on the tide
Nor bid that lonely freighter not
To set out at this twilight hour.

*Translation first published in *The Taipei Chinese Pen* 145
　（Autumn 2008）: 18-19.

蒼茫時刻

溫柔的黃昏啊唯美的黃昏
當所有的眼睛都向西凝神
看落日在海葬之前
用滿天壯麗的霞光
像男高音為歌劇收場
對我們這世界說再見
即使防波堤伸得再長
也挽留不了滿海的餘光
更無法叫住孤獨的貨船
莫在這蒼茫的時刻出港

In Memory of Chopin

For eight thousand miles on my trip to Warsaw
My ear was rainsed with your plaintive tune.
Your childhood house at Zelazowa Wola
I saw at last, a wish at last fulfilled.
What my pilgrim shoes brought back to Kaohsiung
Was the same soil you carried abroad
When you waved your dear Poland good-bye.
Long was the exile road that never turned back.
Unforgettable was the clay that smelt Polish
And the kitchen that smelt of mother. After
Vienna and Munich, Majorca and Paris,
Amid the coughing hardly drowned in mazurka,
Home remained out of reach except in dream.
Twice, since you left, your country has fallen;
The Eternal Town prophesied by the Mermaid
Has fallen again and again in fire.
After all the wars the Warsaw that greeted me
Was not the Warsaw you had bid farewell.
The keyboard, sad as if saying your will,
Was powerless to rescue Poland from ruin.
Yet neither the Russian hooves and boots

永念蕭邦

迢迢八千里初夏的華沙之行
漱耳泠泠是你的琴音
終於到了你故居，了卻心願
被我的鞋底帶回西子灣的
正是你當年告別波蘭
親身帶去異鄉的泥土
不再回頭是浪子的遠路
祖國的泥香，母親的廚房
該都是一樣難忘吧，縱使
從維也納到慕尼黑
從馬佐爾卡到巴黎，琴聲
蓋不住咳聲，也一直在夢裡
你走後故國又滅了兩次
人魚預言的不朽之城
淪陷的劫火噬了又吞
迎我的華沙，唉，幾輪灰燼
早非當日送你的華沙
琴聲再悽惋，像遺囑遺恨
何曾真正救得了波蘭？
但帝俄的馬蹄和皮靴

Nor the Nazi tanks could crush a prelude.

Crescendo goes the Étude of Revolution,

And nocturnes still murmur of George Sand.

When your magic fingers rise and fall

And black keys answer as white keys call,

When staccato and legato windward fly,

The world listens to your song, and, spell-bound,

All the enchanted ears to Poland turn.

For who can ever forget, Frédéric,

One hundred and ninety years old as you are,

The piano you left us remains as young,

As passionate and as mellifluent

As the flowing Vistula that, day and night,

North-bound, still washes your tears and blood.

—1999

*Translation first published in The Taipei Chinese PEN 131
（Spring 2005）: 4-5.

納粹壓境的坦克車隊
也休想壓碎你一首序曲
革命練習曲愈敲愈高亢
夜曲仍放不下喬治桑
當你的修指，敏感地一起，一落
當黑鍵與白鍵一呼，一應
當斷音與滑音在上風飛揚
全世界都在下風聆聽
所有的燙耳都轉向波蘭
誰啊能忘記，佛雷德瑞克
你一去已經一百五十年
而那架鋼琴仍那樣年輕
那樣流利啊那樣盡情
正如維斯圖拉河，日日夜夜
仍朝北流著你的淚與血

——1999

301

The Emerald White Cabbage

—A sculpture in the Palace Museum

Ore-born of Burmese or Yunnan descent
By whose hand, sensitive and masterly,
Driving and drilling its way so surely,
Leaving clean all the tendons and bones,
Are you released from the jadeite jail?
Refined further by the fingers of Jin,
The royal concubine, and polished bright
By the spectators' adoring gaze
Focussed under the light, year after year,
Until a liquid clarity is lit within,
Verdant and pearly, no longer are you
Merely a piece of jade or a cabbage
Since the day the sculptor set you free
And left, instead, his own devoted soul
Reincarnate in the womb of the jade,
Beyond the relentless pursuit of time.
Art is simply play become truth,
Truth at play, even truer than real.
Or why is that vivid katydid,
Unmoved in its faith, still holding on

翠玉白菜
—— 詠故宮雕刻

前身是緬甸或雲南的頑石
被怎樣敏感的巧腕
用怎樣深刻的雕刀
一刀刀，挑筋剔骨
從輝石玉礦的牢裡
解救了出來，被瑾妃的纖指
愛撫得更加細膩，被觀眾
豔羨的眼神，燈下聚焦
一代又一代，愈寵愈亮
通體流暢，含著內斂的光
亦翠亦白，你已不再
僅僅是一塊玉，一棵菜
只因當日，那巧匠接你出來
卻自己將精魂耿耿
投生在玉胚的深處
不讓時光緊迫地追捕
凡藝術莫非是弄假成真
弄假成真，比真的更真
否則那栩栩的螽斯，為何
至今還深信，還抱著

To the fresh green without regret?

Perhaps it's the sculptor in his rebirth.

*Translation first published in *The Taipei Chinese PEN* 127 (Spring 2004) : 22-23.

猶翠的新鮮，不肯下來
或許，那就是玉匠轉胎

Aunt Ice, Aunt Snow

—In memory of two beauties in the water family

Aunt Ice, please cry no more
Or the seas will spill all over,
And homeless will be the polar bear,
And harbors will be flooded,
And islands will go under.
Cry no more please, Aunt Ice.

We blamed you for being so cold,
Fit to behold, but not to hold.
We called you the Icy Beauty,
Mad egoist on keeping clean,
Too proud ever to become soft.
Yet, when you cry so hard, you melt.

Aunt Snow, please hide no more
Or you will truly disappear.
Almost a stranger year after year,
When you do come, you're less familiar,
Thinner and gone again sooner.
Please hide no more, Aunt Snow.

冰姑，雪姨
—— 懷念水家的兩位美人

冰姑你不要再哭了
再哭，海就要滿了
北極熊就沒有家了
許多港就要淹了
許多島就要沉了
不要哭了，冰姑

以前怪你太冷酷了
可遠望，不可以親暱
都說你是冰美人哪
患了自戀的潔癖
矜持得從不心軟
不料你一哭就化了

雪姨你不要再逃了
再逃，就怕真失蹤了
一年年音信都稀了
就見面也會認生了
變瘦了，又匆匆走了
不要再逃了，雪姨

You were beloved as the fairest:
With such grace you used to descend,
Even more lightly than Aunt Rain.
Such pure white ballerina shoes
Drift in a whirl out of heaven
Like a nursery song, a dream.

Cry no more please, Aunt Ice.
Lock up your rich treasury,
Shut tight your translucent tower,
And guard your palaces at the poles
To keep the world cool and fresh.
Cry no more please, Aunt Ice.

Hide no more please, Aunt Snow.
"Light Snow is followed by Heavy Snow."
Descend in avalanche, Aunt Snow!
Your show the Lunar Pageant waits.
Come and kiss my upturned face.
Hide no more please, Aunt Snow.

*Translation first published in *The Taipei Chinese PEN* 142 (Winter 2007) : 3-4.

以前該數你最美了
降落時那麼從容
比雨阿姨輕盈多了
潔白的芭蕾舞鞋啊
紛紛旋轉在虛空
像一首童歌，像夢

不要再哭了，冰姑
鎖好你純潔的冰庫
關緊你透明的冰樓
守住兩極的冰宮吧
把新鮮的世界保住
不要再哭了，冰姑

不要再躲了，雪姨
小雪之後是大雪
漫天而降吧，雪姨
曆書等你來兌現
來吧，親我仰起的臉
不要再躲了，雪姨

Cirrus over Cape Cod

With no excuse at all,

Up across the blue crystal dome

Wafts such a whimsical wisp,

Foamy and feathery, rolling, unrolling,

Like an idle white peacock in doze.

It must be after a long sunny spell

The wind wonders how far it can blow

In one breath and to what ethereal height

It can lift this impromptu kite

To the topmost freezing sphere

Where no eagle presumes his claim.

The angels are all alert:

"This is high enough. The Power

Will surely be offended!"

So it is confiscated.

*Translation first published in *The Taipei Chinese PEN* 145
（Autumn 2008）: 3.

鱈岬上空的卷雲

無緣無故地
高不可攀的藍水晶頂上
忽然飄過來這一綹輕紗
似飛似浮，似捲似舒
似一隻慵懶的白孔雀在午寐
想必是久晴的長風
要測試它一氣能吹多遠
能把這即興的風箏
放到究竟多高的空際
──那樣凜冽的最上頂層
所有的鷹隼都被迫放棄
天使們全都驚覺了
「夠高了吧，夠高了
神快要被冒犯了」
說著，就將它沒收了

At the Dentist's

On the couch not meant
For idle dreams, I have lain,
Ready to lock my teeth
Like a martyr facing the squad,
But was told to keep agape.

Roar, surely, is not allowed
Nor is the tongue certain
Where to turn for refuge.
So the mind is all set,
The eyes closed all tight.

Clicks clear and crisp,
Metallic against glazed plates:
To pick, to scoop,
To file, to rub,
The whole refined torture set.

Suddenly, deep down the cave,
Where the ear has its roots,
Who is driving a power drill

牙關

不容你悠然尋夢的躺椅
已經躺上去
正待咬緊牙關
效烈士之臨難
卻要我大張獅口

吼，是休想吼了
也不知讓舌頭
去何處避難
只能把心一橫
把眼睛閉關

傳來清脆的音響
該是金屬碰瓷盤
或挑，或挖
或磨，或刮
精緻的一整套刑具

忽然迴旋梯底
向耳根的深處
是誰呀用一架電鑽

At such high frequency and pitch
Through all my stalagmites

To rake my corruptions
And search all dark corners
For scandals yet unexposed?
Down the gutter they are flushed,
Gargling, antiseptic.

Torment after torment
Until confessions are wrung,
Until out is spit the whole truth,
The white-gowned judge then says,
"That's all," and sets me free.

*Translation first published in *The Taipei Chinese PEN* 145
（Autumn 2008）: 3-7.

高分貝的頻率哪
在我的牙床開礦

在偵查我的腐敗
捉拿潛伏在暗處
不堪曝光的隱私
地下水冷冷漱過
有一點消毒的藥味

一遍又一遍的刑求
只為了逼出口供
該吐的都吐實了
那白袍法官說
好了，竟把我放了

Arco Iris

The rainbow is Aunt Rain's tearful laughter
That takes the landscape by surprise:
Such a glimpse of revelation!
For whom, indeed, is the door open,
The ladder leaning, the bridge awaiting?

She is my child, says Aunt Rain,
Craving light and water, born of the sun
Whose beams, pregnant once in water,
Flash all across the spectrum.
A wink, and Beauty comes into being!

Fleeting and capricious,
Where is Child Rainbow gone?
The rain says, "She hides in my mirror."
The sun says, "She sleeps in my beam."
The out-bow says, "She nestles in my arms."

*Translation first published in *The Taipei Chinese PEN* 145
（Autumn 2008）: 8-10.

虹

虹是雨阿姨帶淚的笑聲
使風景驚愕，一綻天啟
一扇門，是為誰開闔
一道梯，是等誰下來
一座橋，是接誰上去

雨姨說，虹是她的孩子
嗜光，嗜水，為日神而生
光入水而成孕
睽睽七色的眼神
一回頭，美，已誕生

出沒無常，明滅任性
虹孩的身世成謎
雨說，她藏在我的鏡中
日說，她睡在我的光中
霓說，她偎在我的懷裡

317

Tug of War with the River

If Time should be a long, long river
With ripples in day and night
And torrents in year after year,
    Over the rushing flood,
Who is calling, then, faintly from upstream?
Who, knowing too well I can't swim back,
    Should be, day and night,
    Calling me to go home?

If Time should be a long, long river
With ripples in day and night
And torrents in year after year,
    Over the rushing flood,
Who is calling, then, faintly from midstream?
Who, knowing too well I can never stay,
    Should be, day and night,
    Calling me to get on shore?

If Time should be a long, long river
With ripples in day and night
And torrents in year after year,

水草拔河

如果時間是一條長河
晝夜是漣漪，歲月是洪波
滔滔的水聲裡
是誰啊，隱隱在上游叫我
是誰，明知我不能倒游
日日，夜夜
卻叫我回家去

如果時間是一條長河
晝夜是漣漪，歲月是洪波
滔滔的水聲裡
是誰啊，隱隱在中游叫我
是誰，明知我不能停留
日日，夜夜
卻叫我上岸去

如果時間是一條長河
晝夜是漣漪，歲月是洪波

Over the rushing flood,
Who is calling then, faintly from downstream?
    Should be, day and night,
    Calling me to speed ahead?

Who is calling, upstream, over the flood?
Who is calling, midstream, over the flood?
Who is calling, downstream, over the flood?
Over the flood, no road upstream;
Over the flood, no ferry midstream;
Over the flood, no bridge downstream;
    Over the rushing flood.

Nothing but the river, torrential ever,
    Rippling day and night,
    Surging year after year.
Me only upon the torrent,
Clinging to the last reed,
To keep up the tug with the flood
    All the way down the river
    From the source to the mouth.

*Translation first published in *The Taipei Chinese PEN* 145
（Autumn 2008）: 10-11.

滔滔的水聲裡
是誰啊，隱隱在下游叫我
是誰，明知我不能抗拒
日日，夜夜
卻叫我追過去

上游是誰在叫我，水聲滔滔
中游是誰在叫我，水聲滔滔
下游是誰在叫我，水聲滔滔
水聲滔滔，上游啊無路
水聲滔滔，中游啊無渡
水聲滔滔，下游啊無橋
水聲滔滔

只有滔滔向東的長河
翻著漣漪，滾著洪波
滔滔的水聲裡
只有我，企圖用一根水草
從上游到下游
從源頭到海口
與茫茫的逝水啊拔河

Great Is a Mother's love

—*to a victim orphaned by the recent earthquake in Sichwan*

Even if heaven falls, Mother
Would shield you with her spine,
Or if earth erupts, Mother
Would shelter you in her arms.
To give you birth, Mother
Exchanged her life for yours.
Doomed and resigned, Mother,
Before she gasped her last
With her indefatigable,
Oh, indomitable will,
Has even defied the whole weight
Of tonnage immeasurable
Under the Himalaya Range
In its mountain-making might.
Too soon for goodbye, Mother
Had to let go her grip
And leave you, helpless and lost,
Calling heaven and earth, calling
—Mother, Mother, Mother

大哉母愛
—— 給四川地震大難不死的孤兒

天塌下來有媽媽
用脊椎來頂住
地翻過來有媽媽
用胸脯來護住
當初生你，媽媽
不惜破胎更開骨
今日救你，媽媽
用她的命，換你的命
苦命，認命的媽媽
在斷氣之前用她
不甘放棄，啊，不甘
不甘放棄的元氣
抵擋億萬噸壓頂
億萬年造山運動
喜馬拉雅的神力
來不及告別，媽媽
就這麼放手而去
留下你，驚惶而無助
叫天，叫地，叫媽媽
—— 媽媽，媽媽

With no answer from any splinter
Of all the rubble and ruin.
Yet you must, good child,
Despite threat of lesser quakes
And hunger, pain, and dread,
Persist in living on,
Not for your own self only,
But for Dear Mother's sake,
Just because she has twice
Given you life, which makes
Your own twice as dear.

*Translation first published in *The Taipei Chinese PEN* 145
　（Autumn 2008）: 12-13.

整座廢墟的瓦礫
一片也不會應你
但是你，好孩子，必須
在餘震的威脅之下
忍痛，忍嚇，忍飢
一路剛強地活下去
就算不為你自己
也要為媽媽盡力
只為了報答，她兩次
把生命給你，因此
你自己要加倍愛惜

A Visitor from Mongolia

I brought a visitor from Mongolia
To the balcony on the eighth floor
To see the sea. Overwhelmed,
He said, "Never have I seen
So much water together." I said,
"Nor can I make out why, at home,
You have more sand than you can use
For camels to print their random hooves."
Thus exchanging, host and guest started
     to laugh
Until both burst into tears.
I said, "On our side we always feel
So much water we have in vain
That strips of land are kept as beach,
And call your great country sea-of sand,
Whether it be all wet or all dry."
Again laughed both guest and host
Till on his back, how menacingly,
A sandstorm seemed to gather,

客從蒙古來

我帶蒙古的遠客
去八樓的看臺
看海。他大吃一驚，
說，「我從未見過
這麼多水在一起」。
我說，「我也不懂，你家
要那麼多沙做什麼
除了亂蓋駱駝的蹄印。」
直到兩人都流出淚來。
我說，「我們這邊總覺得
要這麼多水做什麼，
所以保留了不少水做沙灘
而且把貴國叫做瀚海，
不管它是全溼或全旱。」
於是主客又大笑。
直到他背後，帶著威脅
沙塵暴似乎形成。

And far down against my beach
Tidal waves seemed to lour threat.
At once we held ourselves back,
Dismissing the storm and the surge.
He gave me an hourglass full of sand
And said, "Before Mongolia leaks out
Do come in time to the Sand-Sea."
I gave him wet salt, half a bottle,
And said, "At last the Strait may dry up.
Keep this in memory of our beach."

而我沙灘上似乎
要漲潮。我們立刻
止住沙暴與潮水，
他贈我一滿盒沙，
說，「乘蒙古還未漏完
一定來看看瀚海。」
我贈他鹽水，半罐，
說，「乘海峽還未曬乾
留這瓶紀念我們的沙灘。」

To Chris on His Going West from Denver

—after the style of western ballad

Soon you'll be through snows and clouds,

Through the eternal wakefulness of the rocks,

And the wind will be cold,

And the miles will be white,

And the miles will be black,

Will come in view and out of sight.

Soon you'll be through sun and sand,

Through the eternal dream of the wilderness,

And the wind will be warm,

And the miles will be brown,

And the miles will be yellow,

Will spin in view, round and round.

Soon you'll be through trees and trees,

Through the eternal life of the trees,

And the wind will be cool,

And the miles will be green,

And the miles will be blue,

Will greet your eyes, scene after scene.

送樓克禮自丹佛西行
—— 仿西部民謠

此去你會歷經雪和雲
歷經岩石永恆的清醒
風吹來會發抖
路有時會發白
有時又會發黑
會來到眼前，又退去背後

此去你會歷經日和沙
歷經荒漠永恆的夢幻
風吹來會發暖
路有時會變棕
有時又會變黃
會轉到眼前，一盤又一盤

此去你會歷經樹和樹
歷經森林永恆的生機
風吹來會涼爽
路有時會變綠
有時又會變藍
會迎面而來，一段又一段

And the miles will be short,
And the miles will be long,
And the miles will be up,
And the miles will be down,
And some will come in thought,
And some will go in song.

*Translation first published in *The Taipei Chinese PEN* 145
（Autumn 2008）: 14-17.

路有時候覺得短
有時候又覺得長
有時候要上坡去
有時候又要下降
有的路值得回味
有的路值得彈唱

Midway

The more riotous the cicadas, the more serene it feels.

How many summers it must have been, since I started my final
    countdown?

The longest buzzing of the cicadas only feels like a swan song now.

The tussle with eternity isn't over yet, defeat is anything but certain,

Jostling for more life doesn't guarantee a sure win either.

Enemies I have galore, but more friends, it seems

A more vivacious cohort as well. Fans I have plenty

From far and wide, too. But a rare soul-mate is

Hard to spot. Spooked by the winding corridor of time,

I caught a glimpse of the back of my own shadow

Zooming in and out, bu never as close, though

As the Tri-Family Governor, Mr Five Willows, or the Four Li and
    Du, major and minor

Pal poets from the past who lean so close as to whisper in my ear.

What is freedom if not a smooth heart, observing the norms,

Quoth the Holy Scholar, as if life ought to stop at seventy,

But only because he has not the fortitude to venture farther.

Seven more years have I now scored after turning eighty

And will soon be surprised to wake up to a ninety-year-old me.

For those who must gain a hundred li, really, ninety is just midway:

半途

知了越譟越顯得寧靜
此生倒數，該是第幾個夏天
蟬聲再長，也只像尾聲了
與永恆拔河，還沒有輸定
向生命爭辯，也未必穩贏
敵人不缺，但朋友似乎更多
也更加熱烈。粉絲是夠多
夠闊了，倒是不世的知音
輕易不出現。光陰的迴廊
一瞥可驚，有自己的背影
似遠又疑近，倒是遠古
三閭大夫，五柳先生，大小李杜
卻近得像要對我耳語
自由是從心所欲，不逾矩麼
聖人說到七十就為止
只為更遠他未曾親歷
而我到此八秩有七了
有一天醒來會驚對九旬
行百里者，果真，九十是半途

Forget it. Who cares about the Guinness World Records?
Boos are hard to swallow, but applauses do not necessarily
Scratch where vanity itches.
I have stood in front of the audience long enough. It's time
To ride the accolade train and disappear behind the curtains.
History only sheds its glory backstage.
If my heart remains calm and quiet, perchance
I can still catch a rumbling ride this way on Van Gogh's trip
Across the Langlois Bridge or
Follow the tapping of Dong-Po's walking stick,
Clicking my way out along the wooden bridge.

*Translation by Yanwing LEUNG梁欣榮 first published in *The Taipei Chinese PEN* 175（Winter 2015）: 4-5.

不必了吧，誰稀罕金氏紀錄
噓聲逆耳，掌聲卻未必
能搔到虛榮的癢處
幕前已經夠久了，何不
乘掌聲未斷就退入重幕
歷史在後台才會卸妝
而如果此心淡定，或許
終能趕上梵谷的輪響
轆轆，渡吊橋而來
或許追隨坡公的杖聲
鏗鏗，叩木橋而去

     —— 梁欣榮教授譯

Notes

Seven Layers Beneath, page 24-26: The poem, written when I was teaching at Gettysburg College, Gettysburg, Pennsylvania in the spring of 1965, is so entitled because of the lapse of seven years between my first and second visits in the U.S.

Smoke Hole Cavern, page 28-30: The Chinese call stalactites "stone bells" and stalagmites "stone bamboo shoots."

When I Am Dead, page 32: I left mainland China in 1949. The poem was written in 1966, when I was teaching in Michigan as a Fulbright visiting professor from Taiwan. Names in the last line are those of lakes, one further west than the other, on the Chinese mainland.

The Black Angel, page 38-40: The poem is so composed that the stanzas are grammatically inseparable one from the other: namely, the last line of each stanza, with the exception of the last line of the poem, is a run-on line. One of the few precedents is Emily Dickinson's "I Like to See It Lap the Miles."

Music Percussive, page 46-60: Marco Polo Bridge is a bridge near Peking, where a skirmish between Chinese and Japanese troops in 1937 precipitated the eight-year Sino-Japanese War. "Pavement massacre" refers to traffic tolls during the holidays in the U.S. I was then on my way home, west-bound to take my boat at Los Angeles; hence the changers of the geographical scene from the east to the west coast. The poem was written in 1966; "Here once chanted I," however, refers to the year 1958-59 I had spent as a student at Iowa City. "The month of the yellow plums" refers to May in China, usually the rainy season when cuckoos coo. Ch'ing Ming, literally "clear and bright," is a festival when the Chinese mourn over their ancestral graves early in April. Tuan Wu, the fifth of the fifth lunar month, is the day of the Dragon Boat Festival commemorating the death by drowning of poet Ch'ü Yü an (B.C. 343-290?).

All That Have Wings, pate 64-66: Li Po (701-762) was a great poet in T'ang dynasty. The poem was written during the Cultural Revolution when intellectuals, writers and artists in particular, were universally purged and disgraced.

The White Curse, page 90-92: The original poem has four passages, of which only the first is here translated.

Often I Find, page 96: The "Red Sun Flag" is the Japanese national flag which overran China during the Second World War.

The Death of a Swordsman, page 106-108: "Circulation-stopping" is a term of Chinese martial arts. It is believed that, by hitting certain spots on your opponent's person, you could stop his circulation and thus keep him disabled for hours.

A Folk Song, pate 120-122: Blue Sea is the literal name for the large inland province of Ch'inghai where both the Yellow River and the Long River (the Yangtze) have their sources.

The Begonia Tottoo, page 124: The Chinese map used to look like a begonia leaf.

Passing Fangliao, page 126-130: Fangliao is a small coastal town in Pingtung, the southernmost county of Taiwan and the "fruit kingdom" of the island.

Building Blocks, page 132: Characters of the Chinese language are square in shape. Thus the Chinese used to call them "square characters," which are easily associated with builing blocks.

Nostalgia, page 134: The author's mother, a native of kiangsu Province on mainland China, died in Taiwan in 1958 at the age of fifty-three.

The Night Watchman, page 140: Five thousand years are the rough estimate of the span of Chineses history.

Beethoven, page 142-144: During the insular and restrictive years of the Cultural Revolution, most artists and musicians of the West were censured as decadent and unhealthful. Not only

Confucius but also Beethoven, Schubert, and Mozart were found "reactionary."

The White Jade Bitter Gourd, page 146-148: A vivid representation of the fruit in form, color, and texture, this splendid piece of sculpture is in the collection of the Palace Museum in Taipei. Nine Regions refers to historical China in her ancient political divisions.

When Night Falls, page 158-160: "Whispering ghosts up on the walls" refers to the Chineses belief that divinities and spirits, though invisible, are always present just three feet over a man in solitude.

Teasing Li Po, page 172: "The Yellow River pouring from heaven" is a famous line taken from Li Po's poem "Let's Drink the Wine," while "the Yangtze goes on to the east" is a line often quoted from Su Shih's poem composed to the tune of "Nien Nu Chiao." Dragon Gate is a narrow rocky passage flanking the Yellow River, often celebrated by Li Po. Likewise, Su Shih's description of Red Cliff, the site of a decisive battle in antiquity overhanging the Yangtze River, has made it popular. Both poets natives of Shu, the ancient name of Szechwan Province, Su Shih (1036-1101) was "the youngster" because he was born more than 300 years after Li Po.

To Painter Shiy De Jinn, page 180: A leading painter from Szechwan who made his name in Taiwan, Shiy De Jinn died in 1981, a few months after I wrote this poem. The doctor had predicted that he was dying of cancer, a diagnosis known to his friends and calmly accepted by himself. The poem was published soon after its composition and was well received by the painter, contrary to my misgiving that he might be offended. Hsü Pei-hung was one of the forerunners of modern Chinese painting. Scenes in the third stanza, so typical of southern Taiwan, were made immortal in Shiy's masterly landscapes.

Summer Thoughts of a Mountaineer, page 184-196: These small pieces are truly reflective of my happy and leisurely mood, in the summer of 1982, on the beautiful, almost pastoral campus of the Chinese University of Hong Kong, where I lived during 1974-85. The train in the last piece passed below my window nightly on the Kowloon-Canton railway, with a distant trailing whistle as if to say goodbye.

Once upon a Candle, page 204-206: The author spent his boyhood in a suburban village near Chungking, Szechwan during the

Sino-Japanese War of 1937-45 and has ever since been haunted by nostalgic memories of those years.

Scenes of Kengting National Park, page 220-240: Kengting National Park is located on the southern tip of Taiwan, where the Strait meets the Pacific. Tachienshan, meaning "the big sharp peak," is its commanding landmark. The gray-faced buzzard is a migrant bird from northern China and Siberia, that visits Taiwan annually in October. The philosopher's dream in "The Black-Spotted Butterfly" refers to a story of Chuang Chou the philosopher who dreams that he becomes a butterfly happily hovering among the flowers and, on waking up, finds himself to be the man he is.

Dream and Bladder, page 242: Bear is a reference to the birth of a son: so it is a congratulation to some one who becomes a father of a male child. Bug refers to Kafka's Metamorphosis. Butterfly refers to Chuang-tze, the Chinese philosopher who dreams himself as a butterfly but on waking feels uncertain whetter he is a philosopher who had a butterfly dream or a butterfly who is dreaming as a philosopher.

The Gecko, page 244-246: The gecko is a species of lizard nicknamed "wall tiger" for the ease of its perpendicular climb.

It is also called "palace guard" because the Chinese court used to feed it with cinnabar and, when there were enough of geckoes so fed, they were pounded thoroughly into pulp which, applied on the female body, would keep its color for life. The mark would vanish, however, when the woman had sexual intercourse; hence its effect in keeping the chastity of the harem. There is in Chinese tradition a cycle of twelve years, each of which is assigned the image of an animal: thus a person is believed to be born a tiger or a monkey. I was born in 1928, the year of dragon. Struggle between powerful rivals is often described as "the dragon fighting the tiger." Since the gecko is a (wall) tiger and I am a dragon, we are supposed to be natural enemies.

Mother, I'm Hungry, page 256-258: The poem was written three days after the tragedy of June 4, 1989. Tomb-Sweeping Day is also called Ch'ing Ming Festival, when people mourn over the tomb of the deceased in the family.

In Praise of Hong Kong, page 260-262: The people of Hong Kong were most outspoken in their protest against the June 4th Massacre.

Holding My Grandson, page 272-274: The scene was in New York

in 1993, when I was sixty-five. My first daughter San-san, the
baby's mother, was born in 1958, when I lived in Taipei in a
leafy alley leading to Amoy Street.

No Lullaby, page 280-282: The straits refer to Taiwan Strait that
separated Taiwan from my home on the Chinese mainland for
almost forty years.

Midway, page 334-336: Tri-Family Governor: Ch'iu Yuan. Mr.
Five Willows: T'ao Ch'ien. Four Lis and Dus: The Major Li
Po and Du Fu, also the Minor Li Shang-lin and Du Mu. Holy
Scholar: Confucius, who died at 72. Dong-Po: courtesy name
of Su Shi, a great poet of Northern Song.

余光中作品集 24

守夜人
The Night Watchman

作者	余光中
責任編輯	蔡佩錦
創辦人	蔡文甫
發行人	蔡澤玉
出版發行	九歌出版社有限公司
	臺北市105八德路3段12巷57弄40號
	電話／02-25776564・傳真／02-25789205
	郵政劃撥／0112295-1
九歌文學網	www.chiuko.com.tw
印刷	前進彩藝有限公司
法律顧問	龍躍天律師・蕭雄淋律師・董安丹律師
初版	1992年10月
二版	2004年11月
增訂新版	2017年1月
增訂新版2印	2018年1月
定價	**380元**

書號	0110224
ISBN	978-986-450-100-7

（缺頁、破損或裝訂錯誤，請寄回本公司更換）

國家圖書館出版品預行編目資料

守夜人 / 余光中著. -- 增訂新版.-- 臺北市：
九歌, 2017.01 352 面 ；14.8×21公分. --
（余光中作品集；24）

ISBN 978-986-450-100-7（平裝）

851.486　　　　　　　　　105022451